KU-590-103

"Company coming."

The barge exploded like a cone of thermite, flinging sparks in all directions. The quality of Sawicki energy weapons hadn't degraded during the past fifty-seven years.

An aircar with vertical fans front and rear sailed through the trees on the other side of the blazing barge, ten meters above the ground. The Sawicki crew was focused on the damage they'd done with their bow-mounted weapon.

Guibert and Karg aimed their stunners. They were, of course, far slower than the weapons specialist.

Wenzil swept *her* beam across the aircar. The Sawicki crew began to laugh uncontrollably. The vehicle flipped and disappeared into the trees doing cartwheels.

"Awful!" Wenzil cried as she lowered her stunner to reprogram its keypad. "Try six-six-one!"

"Modifying stunner settings to permanently impair the personhood of native races is forbidden by—" the Mromrosi observer said.

Another aircar slid through the forest, banking between a pair of the larger trees. The Sawicki gunner fired a wrist-thick hose of stripped ions while the vehicle's bow was still a tad high. The face of the bluff shattered. A chunk of limestone the size of a grapefruit dropped onto the Mromrosi.

The rock remained balanced for a moment. The ensemble looked like a golf ball on a furry orange tee.

The Mromrosi fell over. Guibert and Karge had ducked from the ravening burst. Wenzil didn't, so she beat the men to the new target.

Sawickis jumped in all directions from the aircar, shrieking and tearing at themselves as through they'd been dipped in acid. Neither the gunshield nor the vehicle's hull appeared to have offered any protection against the stunner's effect. The car described a half loop, then slammed into the ground under the thrust of its inverted rotors.

"That's the ticket!" Wenzil cried. "Five-four-nine!"

Baen Books By Gordon R. Dickson

Beginnings
Ends
Forward!
Invaders!
The Last Dream
Mindspan
None But Man
The Outposter
Survival!
Sleepwalker's World
Time Storm
Wolfling

The Lifeship (*with Harry Harrison*)

Created by Gordon R. Dickson
The Harriers: Of War and Honor

THE HARRIERS

BOOK TWO: BLOOD AND WAR

Created by

GORDON R. DICKSON

with

DAVID DRAKE

CHELSEA QUINN YARBRO

CHRISTOPHER STASHEFF

BAEN

THE HARRIERS: BLOOD AND WAR

This is a work of fiction. All the characters and events portrayed in this book are fictional, and any resemblance to real people or incidents is purely coincidental.

Copyright © 1993 by Bill Fawcett and Associates

All rights reserved, including the right to reproduce this book or portions thereof in any form.

A Baen Books Original

Baen Publishing Enterprises
P.O. Box 1403
Riverdale, N.Y. 10471

ISBN: 0-671-72181-X

Cover art by Nan Fredman

First Printing, August 1993

Distributed by
SIMON & SCHUSTER
1230 Avenue of the Americas
New York, N.Y. 10020

Typeset by Windhaven Press, Auburn, N.H.
Printed in the United States of America

Contents

THE NOBLE SAVAGES

David Drake

"Ah, Guibert," said Officer Commanding (with Special Authority) McBrien from the depths of his malachite-lined office. "So glad you could make it. We don't chat often enough, you and I."

Right, thought Guibert. *My direct superior through about twenty levels of Magnicate bureaucracy "asks" me to his office, and I'm going to decide to wash my hair instead?*

The gold crests which dotted the malachite's ugly green were probably copied from McBrien's armorial bearings. Guibert's team joked that the Grand Harrier OC traced his ancestry back to Adam—though McBrien would have been offended at a comment that smacked of Patriarchal Religionism.

Author's Note: Poul Anderson is in no way responsible for this work; however, certain plot elements are a direct result of my reading his excellent *Planet of No Return* (aka *Question and Answer*) thirty-odd years ago.—DAD

"Ah—" said McBrien. *He was nervous. Certainly not of me, a scruffy Petit Harrier team leader.* "Will you have a drink, Guibert? I've got a darling little liqueur from—"

"No thank you, sir." The huge office was filled with ancient and valuable furnishings. Guibert felt an urge, quickly suppressed, to undo his fly and take a whiz into one of the ormolu vases flanking the doorway.

"Ah," McBrien repeated. He was a tall man, straight-backed, with the aquiline face of a Roman consul. (There were probably Roman consuls in his chain of descent too.) "Well, Guibert, would you like to sit down?"

"No thank you, sir."

McBrien's aristocratically pale visage flushed. "Sit *down*, Guibert!"

The chairs were Mission Style, black oak and leather. Guibert settled himself on one gingerly. It was so uncomfortable that it made him think of the cycle of torture and counter-torture which the Spanish and aboriginal cultures had inflicted on one another during the Mission Period.

"Ha-ha," McBrien said. "Sorry if I sounded abrupt, my good fellow. Pressures of command. I'm sure you know, being a commander yourself."

Commander of a four-man Petit Harrier insertion team and the commander of the Magnicate dreadnought *Night-Blooming Cereus*, the most powerful vessel in anything up to fifty light years. *You bet, obvious parallels.*

Speaking of Spanish/Aboriginal culture,

McBrien's grin could have modeled for a sugar skull on the Day of the Dead celebrations. *Would that be Patriarchal Religionism—or an Aspect of Native Culture and therefore a compliment to the OC?*

"Ah," McBrien said. "You're sure you wouldn't like . . ."

Guibert wouldn't. Guibert was going to speak when ordered to, period. Guibert didn't have a clue about what he was doing in the OC's office, and he had a nasty suspicion that he wasn't going to be any happier about the situation when he learned what it was.

McBrien pursed his lips. He tented his fingers before him, then flattened his hands on the gleaming desktop in horror. He'd realized that he might have been thought to be indulging in prayer. Guibert waited, imagining wistfully though without real hope that the Grand Harrier would suddenly dismiss him.

"To tell the truth," McBrien lied brightly, "I've been thinking to myself, 'You know, Guibert looks like he needs some leave.' As a matter of fact, your whole team looks like it should have some time off, Guibert. You and, and . . ."

"Dayly, Karge, and Wenzil, sir?" Guibert said, volunteering information for the first time since he entered the OC's office. "Leave?"

McBrien relaxed visibly. "Exactly! Well, that's settled. I'm sure you gentlepersons will have a wonderful time on Sawick, a *wonderful* time. Have your team ready to go in half an hour, won't you? That's a good fellow."

Guibert blinked. "Sawick, sir?" he said. "Why

in the name of the Nurturing Motherforce do you think we'd want to go there?"

McBrien drew himself up haughtily. He sniffed, a long sound in a nose as aristocratic as his. "Sawick is a favored destination among the *cognoscenti*, Guibert," he said. "Sawick provides a chance to view the sort of natural paradise from which our ancestors, sadly, turned millennia ago. The loss of that innocence is the root cause of the trouble and strife which have plagued our unfortunate race ever since."

Guibert rubbed his temples as if he could massage some sense out of his commanding officer's words. Sawick had been discovered by Magnicate vessels only a few decades ago. It was some sort of nature preserve. The autochthones, cave-dwelling troglodytes, had put all but a few hectares of the planet off-limits to outsiders. The Emerging Planet Fairness Court saw to it that Magnicate citizens obeyed the local decision.

"Many thanks for your suggestion, sir," Guibert said carefully, "but I think my team"—*most assuredly including the team leader*—"would prefer Port Jennet as a leave destination. Port Jennet has many educational aspects of its own."

For example, the act Big Liz performs using a 2-liter beer bottle as a prop.

"Nonsense," McBrien said forcefully. "You'll want to better yourselves, I'm sure. I'm *sure*."

He pursed his lips again. "Besides," he added in a voice that was suddenly as thin as if he were speaking only on one sideband, "it occurs to me that you might be able to do me a little favor while you're there. Ah—"

McBrien stared pensively at his paperweight, an ancient gold statuette which had once tipped the scepter of a West African king. The image consisted of a fat man gorging himself while an emaciated man looked on. The tableau illustrated the native proverb that, "The man with food eats, and he owes nothing to the man with no food."

"A way to save on paperwork, don't you know, old chap?" the OC resumed with the same determinedly-false brightness as earlier. "Don't you just *hate* needless paperwork?"

Does a bear shit in the woods?

But if the brass are telling lies, it's no time for peons to stick to the truth . . . Guibert raised an eyebrow and said, "Action without organization is action wasted, sir. I'm sure you don't imagine that I or any other Petit Harrier would violate proper procedures."

McBrien's smile now looked like the rictus of a man being garroted. "Of course," he said, "of course. But since you'd be on leave and I *don't* believe that this little matter was deemed worthy of a formal report . . ."

What little matter?

Guibert didn't open his mouth, knowing that his best chance of getting out of this was not to get in to begin with. He crossed his hands neatly in his lap and focused his eyes on the OC's beard-fringed chin.

"Ah . . ." said McBrien with a hopeful intonation. Guibert kept his eyes fixed and his lips together.

McBrien sighed. "The fact is," he said, looking at the gold paperweight again, "some young people—dependents of some of the dreadnought's personnel—borrowed a vessel from the *Night-Blooming Cereus*. My cutter, in fact. They, ah, wanted to visit Sawick. No harm done, of course."

Guibert blinked again. "No harm done?" he repeated incredulously. "Punks steal the OC's cutter—*filled* with top-drawer electronics—and they take it to a generally proscribed planet? And there's no harm done?"

"They aren't punks," McBrien said to the paperweight. The words were barely audible because his lips were so tightly compressed. "And anyway, the problem is that they, ah . . . seem to have disappeared."

"Benign Female Principle!" Guibert cursed. "The natives grabbed them, you mean?"

He tried to remember what he'd heard about the Sawickis. If he had the aliens right in his mind, they were humanoid but pasty, stunted and stone-blind. Sawick wasn't a place Guibert or anybody he wanted to know would pick for a local romance.

"Well, there's no evidence of that," McBrien said. "In fact, the Sawickis don't have any recollection of the ah, youngsters. Landing control personnel—Magnicate citizens—say the cutter took off from Sawick but suddenly vanished from their screens. I'm afraid that there may have been a, a . . ."

He looked up. "I'm not really sure what might have happened. But I thought, you know, since you and your team are going to Sawick anyway . . . ?"

Guibert shook his head. "Negative," he said. "Sir."

He cleared his throat. "Sir, with the sort of equipment built onto an admiral's cutter, and Sawick being a Class—what, Thirty?—world—"

"Thirty-two," McBrien agreed sadly.

"Great, Class Thirty-two, with a technology level that's almost but not quite up to the spoon stage," Guibert said. "Either the cutter blew up— or you've *got* to put out a full-dress alarm to prevent the autochthones from being infected."

McBrien shivered as though he'd just come out of a bath in ice water. "Oh, I don't think it's so very great a problem, old chap," he said in his single-sideband voice. "The Sawickis are so safe in their pre-industrial purity that I can't imagine them coming to harm. And a fuss, you see, might cause problems for those poor, misguided young people, don't you know?"

Guibert nodded grimly. "You bet," he agreed. "Like spending the next ten years in a Cultural Re-Education camp when the Mromrosii and the rest of the EPFC hear about what they pulled. And you know, for a change, I think I might agree with the Mromrosii."

McBrien pressed his fingers together. This time he didn't jerk them apart when he noticed what he was doing. "Guibert," he said, "I'd really like it if you and your team looked into this unofficially."

"Not without a direct order, sir," Guibert said. "Because me and my people would wind up hoe-ing rice paddies alongside the punks if we got caught covering up a thing like this."

McBrien bowed his head. "Guibert, do you want me to beg?" he whispered.

"No, sir," Guibert said. "I want you to dismiss me, so that we can both forget we ever had this conversation."

"Guibert, my daughter Megan took the cutter. With seven of her friends."

OC McBrien stood up. He was normally a graceful man. This time there was a dangling looseness about him, like the motions of a scarecrow being hung on a pole. "If you won't take care of this, Guibert," he said, "then I'll have to go myself. Unofficially."

"Sir," Guibert said. "Sir, with all due respect, a Grand Harrier trying to act outside the system would screw things up beyond reasonable belief."

McBrien nodded. "Yes, Mister Guibert," he said. "I'm very much afraid you're right."

"By the Menstruation of the Life-Giving Yang," Guibert muttered as he got to his feet. "Sir, I'll talk to the team. No promises, but I'll talk to the team."

He'd order the team. It was his decision, he was in charge. And anyway, they were professionals. A pro doesn't sit around and watch an amateur make a bad situation worse.

"But one thing!" Guibert added sharply from the door. "*If we do this*"—*and if we don't get our butts confined in a re-education camp till all of us but Wenzil are tripping on our beards*—"then we get a *real* leave out of it. On Port Jennet!"

The Grand Harrier nodded assent. Even under

the present circumstances, McBrien couldn't avoid a moue of distaste at the idea of personnel under his command having fun.

" . . . so we'll be going down in a standard leave barge," Guibert explained to his team. "We'll have a full set of orbital scans, but no special equipment aboard."

"A leave barge!" Karge muttered, knuckling his curly auburn hair. "Typical of a faggot like McBrien to expect us to carry out his mission with a bare hull and an engine."

"We'll play it by ear," Guibert said mildly. "If it turns out we need more hardware, then I'll see about getting it."

He cleared his throat. "Dayly," he asked, "what have you got on the Sawickis?"

Wenzil, the team's weapons specialist, was about average height for a human female—a meter sixty-five. Dayly, the data systems specialist, was both shorter and slighter by 10%. He touched a key and projected a hologram of an average Sawicki above the console.

"Great," Karge said. "So now we know that Sawickis are toads."

Guibert pursed his lips. "Slugs, wouldn't you say?" he offered.

Wenzil glanced up, then returned to what she was doing. She'd stripped the team's stunners on her bunk. She was cleaning the contacts individually with an arc-and-vacuum unit and replating when she deemed it desirable.

It was the sort of task normally performed at armory level or above. Wenzil did it before every mission, and once a week or so when the team was on stand-down.

"What sort of stunner setting does the data bank suggest?" she asked as she peered critically at the main buss from Karge's weapon. "*Not* that I'd trust the data bank, but for a place to start."

Dayly clicked to the end of the file rather than scrolling down. He knew that out of squeamishness, the folks at Central Records would wait as long as they could before stating the information that any sane member of an insertion team wanted right up front: how to program their stunners to have an effect on local lifeforms.

"It says eight seventy-three," Dayly offered in a neutral tone.

The setting was almost certainly extrapolated rather than arrived at by empirical testing on the autochthones. Wenzil was likely to get very upset when her darling stunners didn't perform as she desired. Dayly didn't want to have any more association with a probable mistake than was necessary.

"Hmm," Wenzil said as she punched the code into the stunner she'd already reassembled. "They think Sawickis are slugs, all right, but sea slugs. This is a normal-atmosphere world, isn't it?" She didn't sound concerned, just interested.

"Within parameters," Guibert agreed. "A little high in noble gases, but still under two percent. The figures must be based on Sawicki physiology."

The trouble with stunners was that there were literally billions of life-forms in the known universe. A stimulus that had a stunning effect on one creature might not touch another—or might goad it to fury. Beasts as similar as Terran horses and dogs reacted in violently different ways to would-be knockout drugs.

And, of course, the difference between an incapacitating dose and a lethal dose was often less than a standard deviation within members of the same species. Central could be expected to err on the side of safety—for the hostile autochthones.

"Stunners have got to be the stupidest idea since faculty tenure," said Karge, the ethnology specialist. "It was probably some flaming queen like McBrien who mandated them."

"What we ought to have," said Wenzil, "is *real* weapons. If you blow a hole clear through something, you can be pretty sure it stops chewing your leg off."

"But that would be wrong," the other three team members chorused, "and the Mromrosii wouldn't like it!"

"Thank the Beneficent Flow of the All-Mother," Guibert said, "that at least we don't have to take a Mromrosi with us into this mare's nest."

The door to the team's compartment was locked. It opened anyway. A Mromrosi glided in on tiny feet hidden beneath the train of bright orange hair. The creature looked like an extremely steep-sided orange haystack a meter and a quarter high. Its single eye glinted at Guibert from behind a veil of hair. "What is our departure time, team leader?" it demanded.

The alien had a pleasant baritone voice. It sounded more human than OC McBrien did when he got nervous.

"Ah," Guibert said. He wondered if the syllable sounded as silly from him as when the Grand Harrier spoke it.

Karge leaned forward. "You won't need to come along this trip, Hairball," the big ethnologist said gently. "We're going on leave."

"I know all about your mission," the Mromrosi responded. "An attempt to carry out a mission without the presence of a representative of the Emerging Planet Fairness Court would lead to cultural re-adjustment for the perpetrators."

"You know," Wenzil said wistfully, "there are times I think I might quite like hoeing a rice paddy for the rest of my life. But I'd want the sentence to be for doing something interesting . . ."

She eyed the Mromrosi. Guibert didn't know whether or not the alien could read Wenzil's speculative expression accurately, but as team leader he didn't want to take chances. "Go on with your description of the autochthones please, Dayly," he said in a loud voice.

The data specialist turned to his console again. "Average height a meter fifty," he read in a singsong voice. "They live underground, growing fungus which they feed on decomposing vegetation which they gather from the surface during the hours of darkness."

"They can't stand sunlight?" Guibert asked.

"Now I wonder whether an eight-seven-three setting might not give me lower dispersion. . . ." Wenzil murmured as her attention returned to the numerical programming pad on the receiver of the second stunner.

The Mromrosi's eye rotated to fix Wenzil with its warm brown glare. "You must not depart from Central's recommended stunner settings!" the creature said. "You might *harm* an autochthon by such experimentation!"

"Please, Hairball," Guibert said primly. "Your interference with this briefing could cause one of us to make a mistake that would injure the indigenes with whom we come in contact."

It was impossible to tell Mromrosii apart except by hair color, and Karge insisted that they were able to change *that*. Further, the ethnologist didn't bother trying to pronounce names which he believed the Mromrosii picked at random. Since he got away with it, the rest of the team had picked up the habit also.

The Mromrosi's eye turned again. Guibert wasn't sure whether the whole body moved, or whether the eye slid across the alien's skin beneath the layer of hair.

"I apologize," Hairball said. "Continue."

"They can stand sunlight for a little while," Dayly said, "though they don't have any melanin or the equivalent in their skin, so they sunburn easily."

"You were right, chief," Karge said. "Slugs, not toads."

"The main reason they don't come out by day is that they don't have eyes as such," Dayly continued. "There's a modulated light emitter on top of their heads—a bioluminescent laser, for all practical purposes. There are pick-ups all around the body at neck level, giving them very precise *active* ranging—but in daylight they're at a disadvantage to creatures which have passive receptors."

"Eyes," Guibert translated aloud.

"Eyes," Dayly agreed. "Also, they have excellent hearing."

"Just how strong a laser are we talking about?" Wenzil asked with an intonation that Guibert couldn't initially place.

"Microwatts," Dayly said. "No danger at all."

The weapons specialist nodded sadly. "It probably wouldn't function if it were removed from the autochthon anyway," she said.

Hairball's eye snapped around, but the Mromrosi kept silent this time.

"The Magnicate made contact with Sawick forty-one years ago," Dayly said. "The autochthons were classified Thirty-two and were informed of their rights under the Emerging Planet Fairness Regulations. The Sawickis elected to eschew outside contact except at one village, the Big Grotto, where they've constructed a surface-level nature area as well. Sawick is believed to be very sparsely settled, but the terms of the autochthonal election make it difficult to determine the amount of sub-surface development."

"Slugs living under rocks," Karge said. "Just the sort of thing you'd expect a pansy like McBrien to get us into."

This wasn't helpful. "Look, Karge," Guibert said. "The only thing I know for sure about the OC's private life is that he's got a kid. Right?"

"Big deal," Karge said. "So did Oscar Wilde. He's a poofter, trust me."

"They sell handicrafts at Big Grotto," Dayly said. "And there's lodging on the surface there." He squinted at the screen. "If these prices are right, I'm not going to be able to afford more than three nights on Sawick."

"I'll talk to his parentness," Guibert said. "Anything more?"

Dayly shrugged. "Nothing too striking in the local wildlife," he said. "Frankly, there wasn't much interest in the place except from nature freaks till the kids went missing. The scans done since would have showed up the cutter, though, no matter how small the bits it smashed into."

Guibert sighed. "I guess we're ready when you get the hardware put back together, Wenzil," he said.

Hairball scanned the insertion team one by one. "This should be very illuminating for you," the Mromrosi said. "Try to open your hearts and appreciate the differentness of this pure people, the Sawickis, who live at one with Nature. *True* nobility!"

"Blind, white slugs," Karge muttered. "With arms and legs."

The landing field serving the Big Grotto was paved with crushed stone. The sharp tang of quicklime made Guibert sneeze when he opened the hatch.

"Gesundheit," said Dayly.

Hairball looked at the data specialist. "Are you demonstrating subservience to Patriarchal Religionism, Harrier?" the Mromrosi asked suspiciously.

"No, no," said Karge. "Simply an Aspect of

15

Native Culture. It's a charm against the possibility of our leader expelling his soul along with the sneeze."

"Ah," said the Mromrosi.

"Gee, I didn't know that," Dayly said.

From orbit, the landing field was a six-pointed star, brilliantly white against the dark green and russet of the forest covering most of the continent. A dozen ships, all of them Magnicate designs, were already on the ground. Two of them were medium-sized cruise liners.

"Come along!" a high-pitched voice called. Guibert looked out and saw his first autochthon. "If you miss this coffle, you'll have to wait till the next ship lands. We're certainly not going to waste an escort on a mere four of you."

Sawickis really *were* slugs, though their faces were broad and toadlike and the fleshy peak that held the laser-ranging organ could have passed for a dunce cap. This one, presumably a guide, wore a brown tunic made of something like bark cloth. It was decorated with geometric designs in black batik.

Guibert hopped to the warm gravel. Twenty-odd humans, roped together, waited at the edge of the field. Two of the four pasty autochthons accompanying the group carried meter-long prods with stone tips.

"Actually," Guibert said softly, "there's five of us." The boots of the insertion team crunched down behind him, followed by the vague whisper of Hairball's miniature feet. "And I didn't catch what you meant about 'coffle.' We're Magnicate officials on leave, you see."

16

Ignoring the team leader, the autochthon bowed low to Hairball. "Illustrious sky-brother," the Sawicki said. The creature's voice was unpleasant even when he was obviously trying to be unctuous. "Welcome to the only true world. On behalf of my people, I grant you the status of an honorary Sawicki."

Hairball fluttered in what Guibert supposed was the Mromrosi equivalent of a bow. "Thank you," he said. "Thank you. I am truly honored."

"Naw," Karge said after a critical glance at the Mromrosi. "You don't look a bit like a toad, Hairball."

"Maybe under the fur?" Dayly suggested.

The Mromrosi looked at them. "Sawicki means 'True Person' in their language," he said.

"Somehow," Guibert said, "I would have guessed that. Now, what's this coffle business?"

"Come along, come along," their guide demanded. "You're keeping me and my fellow True Men waiting."

He headed toward the line of humans at a lurching trot. The Sawicki wore boots made of a heavier version of the tunic material. His feet turned slightly on the gravel surface, though it seemed level enough to Guibert.

Hairball followed, drawing the team along behind him. "To prevent visitors from damaging the delicate ecology of this planet," the Mromrosi called over his shoulder, "the Sawickis link individuals together so that they won't leave the prescribed path. A *very* far-sighted regulation, I must say."

"What's delicate about this place?" Dayly asked. "It looks pretty normal to me."

17

The trees were of a number of species, all with noticeably conical trunks which suggested they had less stiffening material per unit of mass than Terran varieties. The branches were whiplike and small-leafed; the undergrowth tended to spike rather than spread.

"*All* ecologies must be carefully overseen to keep them in balance," Hairball said stiffly.

True enough. Nature herself was never in equilibrium. Only outside intellects tried to restrain the natural appetite for change. Usually badly.

"Do you suppose I could check my settings on some of those critters, sir?" Wenzil asked with more optimism than hope. She pointed with her left hand toward a bright-eyed creature clicking at the team from a scaly treetrunk.

"Certainly not!" Hairball said.

"Of course not," Guibert said. "What's that going to tell you that you need to know, Wenzil? It's no longer than your forearm and it seems to be an amphibian anyway!"

All the local life-forms Guibert noticed, with the exception of the Sawickis themselves, were either wet-skinned or chitinous. Some of the latter fluttered among the trees on gossamer wings a meter across. None of the potential targets would help the weapons specialist refine her stunner program. Shooting at them, even with a stunner, would cause more trouble than Guibert needed.

The team reached the tourists. The children were restive or shrieking, and several of the adults glared fiercely at the Harriers. Guibert wondered how long the civilians had been kept waiting.

"Stand here," their guide ordered, pointing to the end of the line. Two of the others grabbed Dayly by the elbows, presumably because he was small, to hustle him into place.

Karge said, "Oops!" and staggered forward, treading heavily on the feet of one of the autochthons. The Sawicki squealed and dropped Dayly's arm.

"Oops!" Guibert said.

The other Sawicki holding Dayly jumped back. Guibert hopped sideways and landed on their guide's foot. The guide squealed also.

"Mister Guibert!" Hairball cried. "Mister Karge!"

The autochthons and tourists looked at the Mromrosi. Dayly kicked the third Sawicki in the crotch and said, "Oops!" happily. The autochthon's squeal was higher pitched than those of his fellows.

The pair of Sawickis with goads moved closer. Wenzil stepped between them and the men of the team. Her hands were empty at waist height, and there was a dazzling smile on her face. The autochthons retreated.

Guibert bent and fingered the rope which tied the civilians together. The tourists drew away from him to either side.

The material was supple, but it seemed strong enough to tow barges with. "Cut from the outer skin of a mushroom that was grown for the purpose?" he guessed aloud.

Nobody responded. Guibert smiled tightly and said to their guide, "I don't think me and the team will need this to keep us on the path. As a matter of fact, I'm afraid it would make us stumble. A lot."

"I promise," Karge rumbled.

Hairball's eye dithered in one direction, then the other. He didn't speak. At last the Sawicki guide said, "Since you're slaves of a True Man—"

He bowed again to Hairball, then winced and rubbed his instep where Guibert had trod.

"—we will make an exception in this case. However, you'll have to surrender the weapons you're carrying to me."

"*This*," said Wenzil, pointing to the stunner in her cutaway holster, "is an icon of my religion. It would violate my cultural personhood to force me to give it up."

"That's ridiculous!" the guide squeaked.

Actually, it was pretty much true for Wenzil. "It would violate other serious strictures as well," Guibert said aloud. "Our, ah, overseer, Hairball, would have us punished severely were we to turn over equipment of such developed character to Class Thirty-two autochthones. It might poison the purity of your, ah, culture."

"I wonder if pearls upset the digestion of swine?" Karge murmured to one of the gaping tourists.

"They're not real weapons anyway," Wenzil said sadly.

The Sawickis' little laser emitters flashed red as they flicked from one member of the team to the next and finally focused on Hairball.

The Mromrosi sighed. "Yes, yes," he said, "I suppose that's correct. A technical matter only, of course—*I* realize that the truth that underpins your culture is proof against such baubles. But regulations are regulations, I'm afraid."

With obvious reluctance, Hairball added, "I will take responsibility for the good behavior of these, these . . ."

Instead of replying, the Sawicki guide turned and called, "Head 'em up and move 'em out!" One of his fellows jerked the cord around the waist of the leading tourist, pulling her down the path.

"I wish you people would learn to behave decently!" the Mromrosi said, glaring at Guibert.

"I wish," said Karge, stretching his long, muscular arms overhead, "that that queer McBrien was here drinking in slug culture instead of me."

They'd walked a half kilometer from the landing field without reaching the entrance to the Big Grotto. The forest's muggy heat made Guibert feel as though he'd been taking a bath in his own sweat.

"I don't see why it's got to be this far," Dayly grumbled.

The data specialist had more work to do during stand-down than the rest of the team. He used that circumstance to avoid compulsory attendance in the Strength through Joy Room—the *Night-Blooming Cereus'* gym. Dayly's cleverness was costing him shin splints if nothing else right now.

"To keep the presence of starships from polluting the village's environment," Hairball said.

"To make the stupid tourists walk their legs off," Karge said.

They came around a bend in the trail. The entrance was in sight a hundred meters away, framed by a yoke made of three stone-headed spears. Either side of the trail was lined with booths from which Sawickis sold a variety of food, drink, and handicrafts.

Tourist children began to shriek and tug against the ropes in their haste to get something to drink. Because some pulled toward the right and others to the left, the line tangled so that no one was able to reach the booths. The autochthonous escort watched, making no effort to intervene.

The team walked over to the booths while shouting parents tried to sort out the mess. Guibert looked at a vat of yellowish fluid. Cups made of fungus caps lay beside it. Local insectoids clustered around the residue drying in the cups.

"Ten hubbles a cup, foreign non-person!" squeaked the Sawicki behind the counter.

"Really?" said Guibert. He took a swig from the straw to the condensing canteen woven into the back of his uniform jacket. For ten hubbles a pop, they could afford to import single-malt Scotch from Terra to sell.

Dayly sniffed the vat. "You know . . ." he said. "I've got a feeling that if I sent a sample of that stuff in for analysis, the lab report would say, 'Your bat has gonorrhea.'"

"You imbibed through your nostrils!" the autochthon cried. "Ten hubbles! Ten hubbles!"

"Pardon our error," said Karge. "Permit me to return your stock to its original volume." He spat into the center of the vat.

One of the escorts ran over to the counter clerk. The two chittered together with a great deal of gesturing. Though the Sawickis faced one another, the lasers in their pointy little heads flicked frequently toward the Harriers.

At last the clerk turned away and pretended to be studying the forest behind his booth. His laser continued to paint the team at intervals as the members drifted down the line of booths.

"You know . . ." said Guibert as he stood before a booth which was selling carved lanterns. "I quite like some of these designs."

"Remarkably delicate handicrafts, aren't they?" Karge agreed. "Remarkable for troglodytes, at any rate. I think upscale boutiques in The Hub might be able to market them."

Dayly cleared his throat. "According to the files," he said, "there's a Big Grotto Trading Association negotiating with Hub jobbers for bulk shipments."

The data specialist looked at the display and shook his head. "I dunno," he said. "Plastic would do a lot better, it seems to me."

Like most of the other Sawicki crafts on offer, the lanterns were made from the caps of large mushrooms, dried and scraped paper thin. The prepared hoods were chiseled into filigrees of enormous delicacy, each one unique.

Internally lighted, the lanterns would be strikingly beautiful. Even now, hanging from the frame of the booth like so many chicken carcasses at a butcher's shop, they had a "natural" loveliness greater than that of the surrounding forest.

The Sawicki clerk in the center of the booth looked like a grub poking its head out of a nutshell. He sneered at the humans.

Guibert rotated one of the lanterns slightly to change the angle of the light falling across the surface. The clerk reached out, plucked the lantern from the peg on which it hung, and dropped it behind his counter. He stamped down. The delicate tracery crunched beneath his foot.

"We True Men are above material covetousness, foreign non-person," the Sawicki squeaked.

"Interesting," Karge said as he and the team leader turned abruptly away.

"I wonder what they spend their hubbles on?" Dayly asked. "Besides a first-rate spaceport control system, that is. And salaries for Magnicate technicians to crew it."

"They ought to import food," Wenzil muttered. "Do you suppose they really eat that cat-barf themselves?"

"We've got our emergency rations," Guibert said. "And anyway, I don't think we're going to be here longer than tomorrow morning."

"All right, all right, foreign non-persons!" the Sawicki guide said. "You may untie yourselves now. You will now visit a village of True Men. Then you will be taken to your accommodations among the natural beauty of our planet."

"Everybody's eaten as much as they could choke down," Karge noted. "Or a little more than that." An eight-year-old was throwing up violently at the edge of the trail while her parents—looking rather green themselves—patted her helplessly. The ejecta didn't look a great deal different from the autochthonous soup the child had swallowed moments before.

"Thank the Ennobling Adiposity of the Mother for emergency rations," Guibert murmured.

"Come along!" repeated the guide. He and his fellows began prodding tourists toward the entrance to the grotto, using knuckles and goads. The pasty-faced autochthons gave the team a wide berth.

Hairball peered at the pool of vomit as he passed. "I suppose," he said in what was for him an unusually ruminative tone, "that since the Sawickis respect the lives even of plants, their meals—though perfectly natural—might not agree with digestions trained to freshly-killed food."

"Hey, Hairball," Karge said. "Did *you* bring any rations?" He reached the yoke of spears and kicked it aside.

The entrance to the Big Grotto was a large keyhole in the surface of the ground. A trail, only partly artificial, led down the side of the opening. Several smaller holes in the rock ceiling illuminated the interior with a diffused glow.

The cavern was about a hundred meters wide and at least a half klick in length. Sawickis and scores of tourists moved among the jumbled rock on the cave floor, but Guibert's eyes weren't sufficiently dark-adapted to see details.

"That ceiling—the cave roof?" he said, glancing upward.

"Umm?" said Wenzil who happened to be the person directly behind Guibert on the narrow trail.

"I'm surprised, as thin as the rock looks, that it's strong enough to hold together," Guibert explained. "I'd have expected the whole roof to come crashing down before now. Limestone rotted by ground water doesn't have particularly high tensile strength."

"Hope it doesn't fall while we're underneath," Wenzil said, though she didn't sound concerned. Things that she couldn't shoot and weren't going to shoot her didn't interest the weapons specialist very much.

At the bottom of the grotto, the pale light reminded Guibert of that beneath thirty meters of water. He could see objects well enough, but their outlines were softened by the faint, diffused illumination.

It was a pity that nothing similar could be done about the smell. Guibert at first thought the pong was that of concentrated Sawickis—there were about a hundred of them in sight, working on crafts or (more generally) lounging and curling their lips at the tourists clustered about them.

After a moment, Guibert realized that while Sawickis did stink, their dung stank a great deal worse. The noble autochthons squatted wherever they happened to be when their bowels gave them the signal.

He looked queasily at his feet—found that his fears were justified—and then noticed that the turd was so dry that it crumbled rather than clinging to the soles of his boots.

"Watch where you step," he warned his team.

"That's funny," Dayly said. "The files say they use their shit as part of the compost they grow the fungus on. Here they're just leaving it lie around."

"It's probably contact with outsiders that has caused the breakdown in the normal routine of the Big Grotto," Hairball said. "It's courageous—heroic, in fact—for the True Persons to sacrifice one of their own villages so that other races can be exposed to the purity of their culture."

"Or it's their idea of a joke on the tourists," Karge said. "As a matter of fact, I wonder if this whole place isn't a joke on the tourists. Do we know anything about how the slugs on the rest of the planet live?"

"Negative," said Dayly.

"Certainly not!" the Mromrosi said. "It's quite enough that *one* village be sacrificed to the greed of the Magnicate!"

"Judging by the prices for them baskets and the slush the slugs call food," Dayly said, "I wouldn't say the Magnicate was in the same league."

Guibert squared his shoulders and took a deep breath—the latter which he instantly regretted. They should have brought nose filters as well as emergency rations. "Well," he said, "if I could figure out a cute way to learn about the missing cutter, I suppose I'd try it. Since I can't, I guess I'll go ask the chief what he knows."

"That bugger McBrien could have managed that himself," Karge said.

Guibert cocked an eye at the ethnologist. "Got a better idea?" he demanded.

"Staying back on the *Night-Blooming Cereus*

and playing with myself," Karge said. "Apart from that, no."

A Sawicki male, neither more nor less disgusting than any other Sawicki, sat on a block of fallen limestone in the center of the cavern. Given his elaborately-layered costume and the number of tourists clustered around him taking low-light holograms, he must have some rank.

"Once more into the breach . . ." Guibert muttered as he walked toward the fellow.

He passed near a pair of female Sawickis hacking patterns into mushroom caps with stone burins as more tourists recorded the process.

"That's odd," Karge said. "They aren't any good at all."

He was right. While the works for sale on the surface were craft raised to the level of art, these Sawickis were creating junk along the lines of jack-o'-lanterns butchered by three-year-olds.

"I could chew mushrooms and shit a better design," Wenzil agreed.

"See how contact with the outside has warped these poor innocents?" Hairball said.

"That doesn't," said Guibert, "explain where the *good* work is coming from, does it?"

"Good in patriarchal, anthropocentric terms, you mean," Hairball replied, adding a click that passed for a sniff in Mromrosi terms.

True enough; but not an answer to the question.

Guibert looked at the crowd. "You lead," he said to Hairball.

"Make way for the Mromrosi delegate!" he added loudly. Tourists turned and realized the tickle on the backs of their thighs was frizzy orange hair that *walked*. They hurled themselves sideways faster than Guibert could have moved them had he slammed into the crowd full tilt.

The front rank of tourists around the chief was on its knees, calling questions to the disdainful Sawicki. Hairball stopped and looked upward at the team leader. "To speak to the village chief," he said, "you must kneel. By this act you honor not the personhood of the chief, but rather the planet Sawick itself."

"Here, I'll take care of it," said Karge. The ethnologist pushed ahead of Guibert and the Mromrosi. He turned and dropped his trousers.

"Karge!" Guibert said. "What on earth are you doing?"

Tourists gasped, screamed, or giggled, depending on temperament. The crowd universally moved well back from the Harriers. The chief called something, bringing Sawickis on the run from all parts of the cavern.

"Honoring the planet as the locals do," Karge explained as he squatted. "Taking a dump."

"You can't do this!" Hairball cried.

"When on Sawick . . ." the ethnologist said. "Do as the Sawickis do."

"Mister Karge," Guibert said. "*Don't.* Or you walk home."

"What's going on here?" the chief demanded.

"Well, seeing as he's addressing us directly . . ." Karge said. He stood up again.

The autochthons had halted in a wide circle around the team instead of rushing directly to the chief's aid. Guibert noted that the Sawickis' attitude appeared to be fear rather than anger.

Sawickis were the sort of bullies who wilted when anybody stood up to them.

"Of course, a seven-five-one setting, Marathrustran Bivalves, might throw them into syncope," Wenzil murmured. The weapons specialist seemed as happy as a pig in shit.

"What?" said Hairball. "What?"

Karge refastened his trousers. In a low voice, the ethnologist began to sing a Chippewa song, *"Do you think she was humiliated, that Sioux woman I beheaded?"*

"Some teenagers from a Magnicate dreadnought landed here last week in an eight-place cutter," Guibert said, "and they haven't come back. We were wondering if you recalled anything about them. Sir." *Courtesy didn't cost much.*

"Why should any True Man be concerned with faceless non-persons?" the chief said.

Wenzil turned to face them. "That doesn't sound like an answer to me," she said. The peculiar lilt in her voice made Guibert shiver.

Enough of the implications must have translated that the Sawicki chief said, "The question was asked through the non-persons who run the devil-machines that guide non-person spaceships. We at once held a village council. No one recalled the missing non-persons, since your faces are all the same anyway."

The guide who'd met the barge added, "We prayed that the soulless non-persons had died with minimal pain, however."

"Then I don't suppose there's much we can do here," Guibert said. "Thank you."

The team headed back toward the ramp up the side of the grotto.

"We'll do the nature watch and spend the night in the tourist lodgings," Guibert said. "Since according to the techs in the landing control facility, that's what the cutter did. We're playing this one by ear."

"You know," Dayly said thoughtfully, "he's lying. But lies are information too."

"Yeah," Karge agreed. "And it's information that turd-burglar McBrien wasn't going to have understood."

"Why would anybody pay good money to watch hogs root through garbage?" Guibert wondered aloud as he walked into the male barracks he, Karge and Dayly shared with ninety-odd other men. "Nature area, hell!"

"Ouch!" said Karge, crushing across his biceps the fly that just stabbed for a meal of his blood.

"Damned good money," Dayly agreed. "This all is coming out of official funds, isn't it, sir?"

"That, or out of that limp-wrist McBrien's hide," Karge said.

Tourist accommodations on Sawicki were sex-segregated. Hairball had presumably tossed the Mromrosi equivalent of a coin before deciding to go with Wenzil.

Not that there was much place to go. The barracks were pole frames, roofed with branches. They couldn't have approached being watertight even before their leaves dried up and fell away weeks or months before. The bunks were three-high, with no mattresses or bedding.

Lights were whatever individual tourists brought with them.

"True Men lie directly on bare rock," the autochthonal concierge—warden?—explained to a tearful father with an infant, no bedclothes, and no light with which to pick his way back to the landing field and a ship that might well be sealed for the night anyway.

"Wonder how that slug would like to be laid on the bare rock?" Karge said, fingering the knuckles of his big right hand. He peered at the circle of "floor" in his handlight and added, "Or mud, as the case may be."

Guibert guided the ethnologist toward their rack of bunks. "That's not what we're here for," he reminded Karge.

"Still," Karge said, "it'd be a way to improve my time. . . ."

Dayly sat on the top bunk, running data through the chip reader he was never without. From the team leader's angle, Dayly's air-projected holograms appeared to be chunks of terrain from the orbital scans.

Guibert's rank gave him the choice of accommodations: the bottom bunk, where his subordinates provided more rain cover than the roof did, or the top bunk which would prevent him from being crushed if the whole flimsy rack collapsed. He'd gone for the former, because Karge had picked the middle where his momentum would be low. Dayly didn't weigh enough to worry about.

"Ouch!" Karge said, slapping another fly. He wiped his hand disgustedly on his trouser leg for want of a rag. "They're sticky when they squish, and they seem to like me even better than they do the pigs. This is *not* going to be a fun night."

"Suoids, not pigs," said Dayly as he continued to sort through pictures of forest. "They're native to Sawick."

"Don't tell me I don't know what a pig is," the ethnologist grumbled. "I'm from Lontano, remember? For that matter, I swatted my share of these damned gadflies when I was growing up, too."

Tourists huddled in clots around their fellows who'd brought lights, talking in desultory, often despairing, tones. When they got back to their homes, they would pontificate about the benefits they had bestowed on their offspring by exposing the children to the pure beauties of nature.

Not now, however. Guibert wondered whether some of the fortunate offspring weren't going to be strangled here on Sawick unless they stopped wailing. Not that he blamed the kids.

"Who says the pigs are native here?" Guibert asked. "Dayly?"

"The place was discovered forty years ago," the data specialist said without emphasis. "The suoids are present over the whole continent. Therefore they aren't Terran pigs."

"If insects can live on them *and* on humans, of whom I am one," said Karge, "then they're Terran pigs."

"Is there any other warm-blooded life on Sawick, Dayly?" Guibert asked.

"Sure, the Sawickis," Dayly said.

"Warm-blooded slugs," Karge said.

"Bingo!" said the data specialist. He reached down with his chip reader, making the rack creak dangerously as he did so. "Look at *that*, sir. This is an enhanced infra-red scan, blown up to one to a thousand."

Guibert stared at a hollow cross formed of faint white lines against the dark background. "Yeah?" he said.

"I told the system to sort for anomalies," Dayly explained. "This is what it came up with."

Karge craned his neck to see the display from the correct angle. "It's not the OC's cutter," he said.

"Of course not," Dayly said. "Even the Grands would have found *that*. This is the remains of a village. Trees have grown up over it, but on IR you can still see where the foundations were."

"Well I'll be damned," Guibert said. "The cutter had a complete recon system, didn't it?"

"You think the kids noticed something funny and decided to take a look?" Karge said. "I can't imagine they were satisfied with the entertainment they were getting around here."

"Yes *sir*," Dayly said. "I don't suppose Hairball would let us go take a close-up look tomorrow, would he?"

"Not at a proscribed area of the planet, unless we had direct evidence the cutter was there," Guibert said thoughtfully. "Of course the kids shouldn't have been there either."

"The kids," Karge noted, "shouldn't have gone off joyriding in that faggot McBrien's cutter to begin with."

Dayly snickered. "This means a bunch of

spoiled kids figured out something that the Magnicate bureaucracy couldn't in forty years," he said.

"Does that surprise you?" Karge asked. "Remember, the kids didn't have Mromrosii from the EPFC sitting on their shoulders, making sure truth was twisted into the politically correct pattern."

"Well," said Guibert, "let's see if we can't get some sleep. We're likely to have a long day ahead of us tomorrow, unless Hairball can keep us from having engine trouble at the point I sort of think we're going to."

"Oh, golly!" Guibert said when the altimeter read 30K. "We're losing power! We have only enough thrust to permit me to set down softly."

"I'll engage the emergency alert transmitter!" said Karge cheerfully from the duplicate console. He switched the barge into stealth mode.

Guibert disconnected the barge's AI pilot and chopped the power. Dipping the nose, he started to glide toward the ancient building site. It was a bright, clear day. Inertial guidance and the vessel's passive sensors would be sufficient to put the team where they wanted to be.

The barge's skin formed a laminar path for the optical spectrum; longer wavelengths were scattered or absorbed. So long as the pilot avoided a turbulent wake (ripples in the atmosphere were radar-visible even if the cause of the disturbance wasn't), the vessel was virtually invisible.

The OC's cutter had even better stealth characteristics than the Petit Harrier barge did. Based on the description the port controllers had given, the kids had known exactly how to use their equipment.

Might be worth mentioning to a recruiting officer. Assuming the kids get back. Assuming we get back too.

"Shouldn't we be calling the port for help?" Hairball asked. The Mromrosi's voice remained a calm, dulcet baritone, but he looked twice as large as usual. His orange hair was sticking straight out from his skin.

"What?" said Karge. "You would have us use the manual override to interfere with the automatic alert system? You would have us *violate Standard Operating Procedure?*"

"Well, I—" the Mromrosi said. "Ah—of course those technical things aren't my field, you realize."

"Violate SOP indeed," Karge muttered.

"I'll log the improper request, sir," Dayly said, surprising Guibert. The data specialist was normally too straightforward to pick up on these little games.

Poor guy. Focused on Truth in a society dominated by Fairness.

"Or for that matter, setting three-three-one," Wenzil said, speaking aloud but without real hope that anybody else was interested. "Leonids and Hraunian vertebrates in general. The slugs' serotonin release system might well be similar."

"Hang on," said Guibert. "There may be some tree branches or—"

But there weren't. Guibert fluffed to a momentary hover on the attitude jets a few meters above the surface, then dropped the barge neatly into a circular clearing at the base of a low bluff.

"I do hope the True Persons won't be offended that we've trespassed on their planet," Hairball said. His concern, though real enough, had waited for the barge's safe landing.

"Maybe they've gotten used to it," said Dayly. He'd been watching the visual display without responsibility for the controls. "There was exhaust scarring on the soil. Another ship's been here recently."

"What?" said Hairball. "Trespassers in a proscribed area?"

"I think," Guibert said as he opened the hatch, "we've found the kids. Or at least where the kids went when they left the Big Grotto."

"Now, setting two thirty-six would provide improved range through this atmosphere. . . ." Wenzil said.

She smiled as she led the team out through the hatch. Hairball was uncharacteristically silent.

The air was warm and musty, but it lacked the sour smell that pervaded the environs of the Big Grotto. The Sawicki stench was for the most part confined underground, but the tourists were expected to dump their waste and garbage on a midden. Hogs and bacteria provided the remainder of the reclamation process, neither category an odor-free medium.

"There certainly isn't any sign of foundations from up close," Guibert said. "Did I land us in the right spot, Dayly?"

"Yessir," said the data specialist as he squatted. He opened his field kit and took out a small prybar.

The vegetation was subtly different from that in the neighborhood of the Big Grotto only a hundred klicks away. This forest wasn't quite a monoculture, but the large trees were limited to three or four species. Guibert had noted literally hundreds of different varieties along the path from the landing field, and he wasn't trying to make a detailed census.

"This is regrowth on a cleared area," he said. He walked toward the bluff twenty meters away.

He'd seen the outcrop during landing, but he'd expected that at ground level it would be concealed by the boles of closely spaced trees. The vegetation hadn't had time to build itself into the impenetrable layers that would thin the forest floor by light-starvation.

There was a path from the clearing to the bluff. Trees had been cut or shoved sideways by an object which was dragged through them with enough force to pull up half their roots.

"Well," offered Hairball, "obviously the Sawickis evolved on the surface. These are the remains—you say there are remains—of an early Sawicki village."

Dayly dropped a bit of black material into the isotope separator from his kit and paused for its reading. "Not as early as all that," he said. "Fifty-seven years ago, plus or minus three, from carbonized material trapped under the fused rock."

Karge laughed.

"Fused rock?" the Mromrosi said, utterly at sea. "From a volcano?"

"From an energy weapon," Guibert said. "Somebody blew the center out of a village, then used heavy equipment to break up the rest of it. Most of the buildings were probably wood anyhow."

The face of the bluff looked *almost* right. The join was invisible save for slight differences in lichen cover. The stone beneath Guibert's fingertips felt several degrees cooler than the material that closed the meters-wide hole in the outcrop.

"You didn't calibrate for the Carbon 14/16 ratio for *Sawick's* atmosphere!" Hairball cried in an access of hope. "That's why the date figure you got for the wood is so low!"

"Teach your grandmother to suck eggs!" Dayly snapped, seriously offended by the slur on his competence within his specialty. "Besides, it wasn't wood. It was carbonized bone. Human bone with ninety percent assurance."

"Come here, Dayly," Guibert said. "We've got what's either a plug or a door. If it's a door, I want you to open it." If it didn't open, maybe the barge could push the block out of the way.

"Piece of cake!" the data specialist said. He trotted over, rummaging in his case for another tool.

"I don't understand!" Hairball moaned. From the Mromrosi's tone, he did understand—but he *really* didn't like the implications of what he understood.

"Company coming," Wenzil called.

Guibert heard the sound too, the throb of rotors though the engines driving them were inaudible. He couldn't tell direction or distance through the forest.

"I guess I'll start with eight seventy-three and switch to—"

The barge exploded like a cone of thermite, flinging sparks in all directions. *The quality of Sawicki energy weapons hadn't degraded during the past fifty-seven years.*

An aircar with vertical fans front and rear sailed through the trees on the other side of the blazing barge, ten meters above the ground. The Sawicki crew was focused on the damage they'd done with their bow-mounted weapon.

Dayly was busy with the bluff face, but Guibert and Karge aimed their stunners. They were, of course, far slower than the weapons specialist.

Wenzil swept her beam across the aircar. The Sawicki crew began to laugh uncontrollably. The vehicle flipped and disappeared into the trees doing cartwheels.

"Awful!" Wenzil cried as she lowered her stunner to reprogram the keypad. "Try six-six-one!"

"Got it!" Dayly said. "It's a door!"

Three Sawickis ran out of the trees carrying thick tubes pointed forward from alongside their hips. They and the Harriers saw each other at the same time.

Guibert and Karge fired before the aliens could swing their bulky weapons to bear. The Sawickis hopped about, giggling. One of them triggered his weapon into a tree. A cubic meter of wood vanished in dazzling pyrotechnics. The trunk lifted skyward, then spiked straight down into the soil. Branches tangled with those of neighboring trees kept the bole upright.

Wenzil fired, using her new stunner setting. The

Sawickis went limp and fell, their faces smiling beatifically.

"Not good enough!" the weapons specialist said. "Try five-four-nine!"

"Leave the damned setting!" Karge said. "It's fine the way it is!"

"Into the cave!" Guibert said. "It'll cover our flanks!"

"Modifying stunner settings to permanently impair the personhood of native races is forbidden by—" Hairball said.

Another aircar slid through the forest, banking between a pair of the larger trees. The Sawicki gunner fired a wrist-thick hose of stripped ions while the vehicle's bow was still a tad high. The face of the bluff shattered. A chunk of limestone the size of a grapefruit dropped onto Hairball.

The rock remained balanced for a moment. The ensemble looked like a golf ball on a furry orange tee.

The Mromrosi fell over. Guibert and Karge had ducked from the ravening burst. Wenzil didn't, so she beat the men to the new target.

Sawickis jumped in all directions from the aircar, shrieking and tearing at themselves as though they'd been dipped in acid. Neither the gunshield nor the vehicle's hull appeared to have offered any protection against the stunner's effect. The car described a half loop, then slammed into the ground under the thrust of its inverted rotors.

"That's the ticket!" Wenzil cried. "Five-four-nine!"

Guibert holstered his stunner to pick up Hairball. Karge was bending to do the same. To both men's surprise, the Mromrosi got to its tiny feet unaided. *Little beggar must be boneheaded in pure fact!*

"Come on!" Guibert said, grabbing a handful of orange hair while Karge gripped the Mromrosi from the other side. They ran into the cave, dragging the alien along.

Dayly's electronic manipulations had pivoted away a huge disk of rock-patterned plastic. The data specialist had gone ahead with a handlight; Wenzil would provide a rear guard that no slug was likely to dent.

"My faculties have been seriously disarrayed!" Hairball said. "Nothing I observe would be of the slightest evidentiary purpose in an EPFC hearing."

"Come on, *run!*" Guibert gasped. The Sawickis' energy weapons had forged burnt air and burnt rock into an anvil-hard stench that choked him.

"Particularly my prohibition on setting five forty-nine should be ignored!" Hairball said.

There was a crash of rending metal behind them. The amount of light coming through the cave mouth dimmed. "Wee-*ha!*" Wenzil called. She must have brought down another Sawicki vehicle, blocking the cave's entrance for at least the time being.

The *tunnel's* entrance. The sides were glass-smooth, line-straight, and perfectly round in cross-section. The Sawickis lived underground, all right, but they sure weren't limited to natural caves.

"There's something blocking the way!" Dayly warned.

The far edge of the handlight beam picked out bulk and motion. Guibert dropped the Mromrosi and fumbled for his stunner again. *Were they Sawickis or—*

The relays of Wenzil's stunner went *tickticktick.* Her motto was, "If it moves, you shoot."

A pair of Sawickis in the tunnel ahead screamed like damned souls and began running up the curving rock walls. Each time they overbalanced and crashed down, they rose and repeated the attempt.

The object almost filling the tunnel was OC McBrien's missing cutter. The Sawickis had dragged the vessel deep enough that the mantle of living rock would conceal the cutter from even the most sensitive Magnicate instruments.

The speed with which the Sawickis had excavated such an immense tunnel was amazing. Guibert wondered what they did with the tailings; though with a whole forested planet to work with, the slugs wouldn't have much difficulty in disposing of a few kilotonnes of rock without coming to the notice of orbital sensors.

Hairball was moving normally now. Karge scooped up an energy weapon dropped by the howling Sawickis. "Here," he said, offering it to Wenzil.

"Are you kidding?" the weapons specialist said. "Listen to those screams from up the tunnel ahead of us. I must be getting *klicks* of range on this setting!"

"Help!" called a human voice. "Help," this time by a chorus of many voices.

The cutter pointed nose-first down the tunnel.

Guibert got out his handlight and squeezed by the vessel. It was a tight fit but possible. "Dayly," he called over his shoulder. "Open us a hatch, will you?"

"Piece of cake!"

The Sawickis had bored an alcove into the side of the tunnel just ahead of where they left the cutter. The opening was barred. The tiny red bulb on the metal grill was the only light the ten humans inside the cell had seen for at least a week.

The eight teenagers wearing filthy but extremely expensive clothing were in reasonable shape. They reached out through the bars, babbling demands that Guibert release them.

The other two humans were indeterminate as to age and even sex. They clutched half-carven mushroom caps to their pale chests as though the objects were talismans against the terrors of change.

Their workmanship was intricate and strikingly beautiful.

"Got the cutter open, sir!"

"Then come unlock these bars," Guibert ordered. "We found the kids too."

"The Sawickis aren't really autochthons!" cried a girl with the same cold perfection of visage as OC McBrien. "The planet's called Novy Evgeny! It was settled by one of the first colony ships from Earth. The Sawickis came less than a hundred years ago and enslaved them!"

"Fifty-seven years," Guibert said grimly, remembering the scrap of bone.

"Hold the light for me," Dayly ordered with

the assurance of a workman thinking only of his task. Guibert obediently illuminated the featureless lockplate as the data specialist attached a suction probe.

"The slaves do all the work," Megan McBrien said. Her fellows had quieted now that freedom was in sight. "The Sawickis don't do a thing, not even clean up for themselves. That's why the Big Grotto's so filthy. They can't have human slaves *there*, of course."

"Piece of cake," the data specialist murmured. Tumblers clicked; the lock sprang open.

It probably *was* that easy a task for Dayly. If asked, he would have said that his equipment had done all the work. Which it had. As soon as Dayly had told it what to do.

"Let's get aboard," Guibert said. "I don't want to spend any longer in this place than I have to."

He shooed Dayly, then the released prisoners, on ahead of him. The pair who'd been born on Sawick wouldn't go until Megan put an arm around the shoulders of each and guided them forward.

"The Sawickis put Ethan and Nicole in with us to teach us mushroom carving," she explained. "They were going to keep us here for the rest of our *lives*."

The cutter was crowded with fifteen aboard, but Wenzil kept the non-essential personnel squeezed to the back of the cabin. Guibert dropped into the command seat.

"We can't back out of here," Karge said, his tone halfway between warning and question.

"Too true," Guibert agreed. "Wenzil! Did you

program this boat's stunners to your pet setting?"

"Is the Pope a symbol of Patriarchal Domination?" the weapons specialist replied.

Ship-mounted stunners were identical to the hand weapons in all respects but size. *If Wenzil thought she was getting kilometers of slug-abatement with a hand stunner, what would three hundred times the power do?*

Something that should have been done at least fifty-seven years earlier.

Guibert triggered the bow stunners in a long burst, then keyed directions into the cutter's artificial intelligence. There was no way a human would be able to control the ship with the precision necessary to run through a maze of rock-walled tunnels.

"Hang on!" he warned. He engaged the AI.

Backblast from the jets rubbed the cutter along the roof with a short, nerve-rending squeal as they lifted, but in seconds they'd outrun their own shockwaves. The main screen combined sonics and low-light imagery to project a view of the route ahead. Guibert found it wasn't something he cared to observe at the present speed.

He touched a control. The navigation unit projected a hologram of the tunnel complex, a huge ant farm stretching for scores of kilometers beneath the ground. Rock walls made a perfect medium for echo-ranging. The cutter's sorting system converted the returns into a detailed map.

Someone put a hand on Guibert's armrest.

Wenzil had allowed Megan to worm forward once the cutter was under weigh.

"The Eugeners froze their population and used only appropriate technology," the girl said bitterly. "Five hundred years after they landed, they still lived in a single village. Except for the pigs getting loose, the planet was almost perfectly natural! How *could* the Sawickis enslave such innocent, harmless people?"

"The Sawickis . . ." Guibert said. Half of him was ashamed to be right. "The slugs play by the same rules as the rest of the universe, I'm afraid."

The cutter changed vector. On the main screen, hundreds of humans gawped from among the bulbous fruit of a mushroom farm. The Sawickis visible were rolling and clawing themselves with mad violence.

Another tunnel mouth loomed before the vessel. Guibert gave it a pulse with the big stunners.

"Hey, Wenzil?" he said. "How long before the stunner effect wears off on the slugs?"

"Darned if I know," Wenzil replied. "Five forty-nine's about a thirty-minute dose on Hagersfield Avians, if that's any help."

Hairball made a throat-clearing chirp. "Setting five-four-nine would erode the nerve sheaves of the, ah, interloping non-autochthons," he said. "The effect should be irreversible."

"No fooling?" Wenzil said.

Guibert triggered the weapons twice more for good measure.

"Of course," the Mromrosi added primly, "I am completely unable to observe or synthesize rationally because of my injury."

Something smashed against the cutter's bow. Guibert hoped it wasn't human. The slugs seemed to confine their slaves to fixed locations. Anyway, the object wasn't solid enough to be a problem to the armored hull.

Karge glanced over from the duplicate console. "You know," he said, "it doesn't look to me like there's an opening anywhere in the complex big enough to fit the cutter through."

"We'll make it," Guibert said.

The cutter yawed 30°. Guibert lay on the stunner switch.

"That's good," the ethnologist continued conversationally. "I've got a date for tomorrow night with a tech from Medical Team Five, and I'd really hate to miss it."

"Not the big blond!" Wenzil interjected. She sounded as incensed as Guibert had ever heard her on a subject that didn't affect her specialty.

"No, no," Karge said. "You're thinking of Boxall, and he's far too butch for me. Besides, I don't think he'd be interested. I mean Quilici, the little sweetheart who doesn't look old enough to shave."

The ethnologist shook his head angrily. "A date with Quilici's not something I want to miss because that fudge-packer McBrien can't keep his own house in order.

"Begging your pardon, madam," he added to the girl kneeling between the consoles.

"Hang on," Guibert warned again. As the bow rotated, he fired the stunners for a last time.

The cutter shot up a sloping shaft and into the huge natural cavity of the Big Grotto. Guibert locked out the autopilot and chopped the main throttles. The bow tilted slightly. The vessel quivered, then began to rise on the thrust of the attitude jets alone.

Tourists stared at the sudden apparition from the tunnel hidden at the back of the grotto. Some of the humans were screaming; but not, Guibert was sure, as loudly as the intermingled Sawickis whose sensory nerves were shorting out.

"Sir?" Dayly called in concern as the cavern's roof swelled in the top portion of the screen.

"It's okay," Guibert said, hoping that he was correct. "The ceiling's too thin to be rock. The slugs roofed over a sinkhole to provide a big enough setting for the tourists when the Magnicate arrived."

The cutter crunched against the grotto's roof. It would be plastic, like the tunnel door, and the gaps the Sawickis left to provide minimal light for human visitors would weaken the structure still further.

It had to be plastic.

Guibert slid the main throttles up to their stops. The drive engines boomed, lifting the cutter through the structural plastic with a violent shudder. Bits of rock erupted to either side of the vessel like confetti at a triumphal parade.

Guibert reengaged the autopilot. "Next stop, the *Night-Blooming Cereus*," he said. His team and the freed prisoners, even the pair of locals, cheered wildly.

"Hey, Hairball?" Karge said. "Do you suppose with the evidence we're bringing back, the

Grands'll be able to act without a full Fairness Court hearing?"

"Since my confusion and lack of evidentiary value won't be realized until I have a physical examination in a week or more," the Mromrosi said, "I rather think my recommendations for immediate action will carry some weight, yes."

He made the squealing noise of Mromrosi laughter before he added, "They may well accept my statement that stunner setting five-four-nine is peculiarly suitable to the personhood of the Sawickis, also."

DOWN AMONG THE DEAD MEN

Gordon R. Dickson & Chelsea Quinn Yarbro

Forty years after
Of War and Codes and Honor

1

Code-crossed orders hand-carried from the Fleet Commodore arrived at *Semper Rigel* late into the Earth Standard night, and were not sent by zap and delivered by Bunter in the usual way but instead were carried by a young Group Leader fresh from The Hub of the Magnicate Alliance who wore the badges of the Petit Harriers with the self-conscious pride of a first assignment.

Line Commander Gilyard Fayrborn growled at his Bunter when it came to wake him, then stirred his hands through his putty-colored hair as the start of his waking ritual. He felt disoriented on the huge ship and wished he were back on his Glavus-class skimmer *Yamapunkt*, with its complement of forty-six Petit Harriers instead of this behemoth of a craft needing thousands to keep it going. Or better yet, a Grand Harrier Bombard with a complement of one-hundred-fifty-six men. He stared at his Bunter as his eyes came reluctantly into focus. He was in no mood for surprises, particularly those originating with the Fleet Commodore. "What is this all about?"

"I don't know, sir. The messenger has the information you seek; I was not given any." The Bunter was already setting out his fatigues and preparing his boots, working with its usual four-armed efficiency. Diplomatically, it prompted him. "It *is* urgent, sir."

Fayrborn considered giving orders to modify the basic program of the Bunters so that they would not disrupt sleep; his Communications Leader had offered to do it, but Fayrborn thought it was too much trouble. "Can't one of the others do it? One of the Group Line Chiefs? They could report to me later," Fayrborn mumbled, feeling his precious rest slip away from him.

"You were the one requested, sir," said his Bunter. Being a machine, it implied no judgment in its tone; a human might have shown disapproval or worry.

Fayrborn let out his breath in a combination of a sigh and a yawn, stretching and looking at the time-patch on the ceiling of his quarters. "What kind of hour is this for messages? Are any of the others in the Group being summoned or am I the only one?"

"As a matter of fact, I understand that all five of your Group Line Chiefs are supposed to join you." The Bunter set the clothes at the end of Fayrborn's bed. "But no one from the *Semper Rigel*. This isn't for their ears."

"That's peculiar," said Fayrborn as he lunged out of bed. He hated having his sleep interrupted; knowing that a messenger from the Hub was waiting made the whole thing less pleasant. And the more he thought about it, the less he liked the covert sense of the circumstances. "Why didn't they just zap the orders scrambled? One of the Group Line Chiefs could have handled them. Why send them hand-carried?"

"I don't know, sir," said his Bunter. "Perhaps it would be better to ask the messenger." It had a shower ready as Fayrborn stumbled toward the bathroom. "Don't take too long, sir," it recommended as it adjusted to the temperature Fayrborn preferred.

Fayrborn got in, letting the water wash over him. Sperking zamlots, he was tired. Worn out. More than that: he had run out of nerve, which he dared not admit to anyone. He made himself stand at attention in the warm water. He had no excuse to feel this way, only thirty-six years old, second-to-top in his Academy graduating class, and a native of Victoria Station, at that. He had no excuse for feeling like an exhausted old man—an exhausted *frightened* old man. He was a man who deserved adulation and respect. He was *entitled* to it. He reached for the soap and began vigorously to lather his chest, trying to infuse himself with renewed purpose and animation. When he finished his shower he was as tired as when he began. It was all he could do not to slight the messenger and go back to bed once again. It was maddening, having Kleesticks outlawed: he could use one about now, to soothe his nerves and help him concentrate. Thirty years ago everyone used Kleesticks, but no longer. It wasn't fair. And his own cache of them was depleted. He stepped out to the ministrations of his Bunter, grateful to the machine for its disinterested care.

Ten minutes later he strode into the conference room and found four of his five Group Line Chiefs waiting: Emmelien Goriz (Hartzheim) of the *Reiwald*, Hsuin Xanitan (Xiaoqing) of the *Suidotal*, Pahnahmah Praechee (Punaraj) of the *Sakibuckt*, and Apanali (Kousrau) of the *Ikemoos*. Only Leatris Sventur (Lontano) of the *Daichirucken* was missing, which was unlike her.

"Good morning," he said testily to the four, and received their disgruntled responses. "Sorry to get you up."

"You didn't do it," said Group Line Chief Hsuin, not bothering to cover his yawn. "That messenger did."

Group Line Chief Goriz nodded as she fussed with the horse-head tag on her collar. She was awake but she was grumpy. "And it doesn't help to blame him. He's a flunky. The Fleet Commodore sent him."

Before Line Commander Fayrborn could think

of anything to say, the inner door slid open and Group Line Chief Leatris Sventur came into the room in the company of the messenger.

She looked around, pale and a trifle dazed. "Sorry. The news is about Lontano. Some of it concerns . . . my family." In the chain of command within the group, she was third from Line Commander Fayrborn, coming after Apanali and Goriz. She was also the youngest of the Group Line Chiefs—twenty-nine—by five years, a bronze-blonde woman with intense light-brown eyes, a lithe body and a relentless mind. She had finished fourth in her Academy class only because she constantly debated with her instructors; if she had been more deferential she would have been first.

The messenger looked troubled as he went toward the head of the conference table. "Line Commander Fayrborn?" he asked, offering a proper salute. "I'm Group Leader Gernold Willister, of Hub Command, Petit Division."

"Yes; good morning Group Leader Willister," he said, returning the salute lackadaisically; he barely noticed his Group Line Chiefs. "What's this all about?"

"A problem," said Group Leader Willister, formal and awkward. "On Lontano. It concerns the entire Magnicate Alliance, or so the Twelve have decided. The Emerging Planet Fairness Court alerted us to the . . . developments. They've given us permission for limited response."

"Oh, pog it," said Line Commander Fayrborn. "The Emerging Planet Fairness Court. What do *they* want?"

"The Uth-Mah-Dzern reported the possibility of invasion of Lontano to the Cyi and the Mromrosio just six days ago. They, in turn, reported it to us and the rest of the Emerging Planet Fairness Court. Your ships' Mromrosii will be notified by morning." Group Leader Willister stood at attention though Line Commander Fayrborn dropped into one of the chairs.

"I can't stand those Uth-Mah-Dzern," he muttered. "Say what you want, any species that looks like huge robot three-headed lobsters with built-on extra arms—"

"Line Commander," said Group Line Chief Sventur, cutting off his complaint.

Line Commander Fayrborn shrugged but made no argument. "All right. Carry on, Group Leader."

"There was an . . . incursion on Lontano. It is thought that the source of the problem could be the Basatan'gal. There isn't enough information yet. They—the Basatan'gal—have not agreed to any lasting treaty with any of the space-going species and the Emerging Planet Fairness Court has put them on notice that they are suspected in this action. The EPFC have not yet issued a general warning, but they are prepared to take action against the Basatan'gal if they continue their aggression, if that is what has happened here, as well as granting their support of the Magnicate Alliance making a response to the aggression. A part of your function on Lontano will be to confirm if the Basatan'gal participation is true."

"When you say action, what do you mean?"

asked Line Commander Fayrborn, disliking the sound of the word.

"A partial invasion of Lontano or so we assume, in maneuvers designed to take advantage of the Colony's remoteness, and to sever access to the J'zmallir Trade Routes before other Magnicate Alliance planets are brought into them: that is the working supposition." Group Leader Willister glanced uneasily at Group Line Chief Sventur. "Some areas were very hard hit."

Group Line Chief Sventur drew a shaky breath. "They haven't totaled up the dead yet. Graves's Registration won't be able to get in for another ten days."

"Why is that?" asked Group Line Chief Apanali.

"The Ounou+iu have stated that they wish to conduct their investigation first. As members of the Emerging Planet Fairness Court, they're entitled to such." Which was The Hub's way of admitting that they had to cooperate with the Emerging Planet Fairness Court, like it or not.

"It's on the edge of Ounou+iu territory," said Group Line Chief Sventur, seeing two of the Group Line Chiefs bristle. "They monitor Lontano from time to time."

"How can you stand it?" Line Commander Fayrborn asked. "It's all I can do to endure our Mromrosii, and they're amusing. It's hard to dislike something that looks like an over-grown child's toy. The Ounou+iu, though—they're like big soft sacks with articulated rods sticking out."

"They've been very helpful," said Group Line Chief Sventur, flicking a look of annoyance at

Line Commander Fayrborn. "Lontano wouldn't have been able to make it through the first century of Colonization without their help. I like the Ounou+iu. And I think they look like enormous, floppy-eared, inverted bagpipes, myself."

"So what does the Fleet Commodore want with us, and why not just zap us our orders?" inquired Line Commander Fayrborn of Group Leader Willister, unwilling to discuss the aliens any longer. "Why send you?"

"Because they are not to be seen by anyone but you and your officers," said Group Leader Willister, assuming his most official manner. "They are classified as Most Secret, and are cross-coded to your Most Secret cranial implants. Not even your Protocol Officers can read them."

"In other words, we're doing something the Emerging Planet Fairness Court as a whole or one of its six member species might not approve of," said Group Line Chief Praechee. "The Hub has plans of its own. But what about our Mromrosii? They're members of the EPFC, and they travel with us. They'll have to know what we're doing."

"I don't know anything about that," said Group Leader Willister. "I only know what I'm supposed to tell you and the written information I must hand to you for decoding by your cranial implants, along with getting your confirmation of orders received. The ship will keep a register of the cranial implant activation and I'll require signatures and thumb-prints as well as voice register from all of you."

"So they'll know who to Court-martial," said Group Line Chief Hsiun. "Sounds good to me."

"Hsuin," said Line Commander Fayrborn, making it a rebuke.

"The Fleet Commodore wants you to know that the Grand Harriers have already been dispatched—"

This unwelcome information brought a groan of disapproval from the Group Line Chiefs; Goriz went so far as to make a disapproving face.

"What have *they* got to do with it?" complained Line Commander Fayrborn.

"They've been dispatched to monitor the situation. With alien races involved, it's necessary to have our diplomats ready to negotiate, and they require proper escorts, considering that Lontano is being classified as a conflict zone." With that preparation, Group Leader Willister activated the recorder. "This is an official procedure. File all responses and preserve here at the *Semper Rigel* or with the *Semper Spica*, if she's nearer, and dispatch zap copies to Fleet Commodore Grizmai at The Hub. No other files are to be kept of this discussion."

The recorder dutifully repeated the instructions and exposed finger- and voice-print monitors, saying, "Ready to record this official procedure. Cranial implant recognition registered."

Line Commander Fayrborn stared at the monitors. "Do we have to do it this way? Won't signatures be enough?"

"Not according to my orders," said Group Leader Willister. "Full cognizance records are required. Sorry." He took his stance at the end of the table. "Under the oath of Petit Harriers, you swear to keep secret the details and purpose of your mission, to reveal to no one but the Fleet Commander or his officially delegated deputy the action taken in accordance with the orders you are about to receive, subject to the full penalties for cowardice in the face of the enemy and/or treason."

"So swear," said each of the Group Line Chiefs, placing their hands on the monitors.

"So swear under duress," said Line Commander Fayrborn.

Group Leader Willister ignored this last. "You further swear that you will make no record of the action you take, nor will you report it to anyone except the Fleet Commodore or his officially delegated deputy for any purpose whatsoever for a period of not less than fifty Earth Standard years following the conclusion of the action, and that if any such report is made, you do so under the penalties already stipulated."

"So swear," the Group Line Chiefs repeated, hands still on the monitors.

"So swear under duress," said Line Commander Fayrborn.

This time Group Leader Willister looked disgusted but continued with his assignment. "I may now reveal the orders of the Fleet Commodore." He removed a platen from the front of his uniform and opened it, drawing out several copies of the document he carried. "Each of you must read this, and sign the copy provided you. I have to carry these back to the Fleet Commodore."

As each Group Line Chief was handed a copy of their orders, he or she began to read through the pages, their expressions grave, no one speaking.

"What does this mean—'In the event of discrepancies of purpose with other Magnicate Alliance authorities, these orders will be regarded as having precedence.'" Line Commander Fayrborn pointed out the relevant paragraph. Oh, Soko, for a Kleestick.

"I think it is sufficiently clear," said Group Leader Willister.

"It means that we might have trouble with the Emerging Planet Fairness Court," suggested Group Line Chief Apanali.

"You mean we might have trouble with the Grands, not the Emerging Planet Fairness Court," said Group Line Chief Goriz. "The EPFC isn't going to fault us if we make honest mistakes. The Grands will. They're the ones we have to watch out for."

"Aren't you being cynical?" asked Group Line Chief Praechee.

"Realistic," corrected Group Line Chief Goriz, her features showing no sign of humor.

"Cut it out," said Group Line Chief Sventur. "Let's save that for later."

"Sorry," said Group Line Chief Hsuin. "Lontano's your home. It makes a difference." He finished his copy and set it aside, regarding Group Leader Willister patiently. "As I read this, we're being ordered to become a secret force for the Fleet Commodore. Which may or may not mean The Twelve. He doesn't have to tell us why we're doing this, just that we have to keep Lontano out of alien hands without getting into a war with the Basatan'gal. That about covers it." He looked over at Line Commander Fayrborn. "Did I miss anything?"

"I don't think so," said Line Commander Fayrborn, who had not finished reading the pages yet.
"We're expected to protect Lontano, but not esca-
late the conflict." He set the pages aside.
"Signatures." He took out his stylus and fixed his
sigil at the top of each page, watching as the others did the same.

"Very good," said Group Leader Willister, his
youthful face not yet well enough schooled to
keep from revealing his thoughts. In this instance
he was smug. "The Fleet Commodore will be
grateful."

"If we win and live to report it only to him,"
said Group Line Chief Goriz.

"For fifty years," added Group Line Chief
Hsuin.

"What if something goes wrong?" asked Group
Line Chief Sventur. When there was silence, she
prodded the young Group Leader. "What happens then?"

"I don't understand," said Group Leader Willister, pausing in returning the documents to the
platen.

"What if we can't do what we're ordered to do.
How do we reach the Fleet Commodore for new
instructions?" She waited politely as the Group
Leader pondered her question. "We can't just zap
him and expect an answer, not with these orders.
There is no one assigned for alternate authority
in these orders. So how are we supposed to protect ourselves if things go wrong? It's possible
they will go wrong, you realize."

"That's covered, isn't it?" Group Leader Willister asked after a short silence.

"Not what to do if we need new orders," Group Line Chief Sventur persisted. "If we act without being in accord with the orders, then we're going against our oaths. But there may be unforeseen hazards. We need some way to reach the Fleet Commodore, or his official deputy."

Group Leader Willister shook his head slowly. "That isn't possible." He fixed the platen to his chest once more. "Follow your orders. They cover the situation." He came to attention; the others stood.

"I want to register one official question," said Group Line Chief Sventur.

"For pogging sake, Sventur—" Line Commander Fayrborn began.

"Just one. If you'll be good enough to record it?" she said to Group Leader Willister, and waited while he activated the monitors once more. "If we're forced to take actions not covered in our orders, who will be responsible for the outcome?"

"That's a poggermox question, Sventur," muttered Line Commander Fayrborn, annoyed.

"Your question is recorded, Group Line Chief," said Group Leader Willister. "If there are no other questions?"

Line Commander Fayrborn gestured his compliance. "We'll be ready to depart at seven." That was too little sleep, he thought, but the orders stipulated the time. He longed for an excuse to refuse the mission, but none came to mind. "All six Glavus-class skimmers, on the most direct route to Lontano." To him his words sounded like the knell of doom.

*   *   *

Group Line Chief Sventur sat with Group Line Chief Goriz in the far corner of the Officers' Mess, steaming cups set on the table before them. The messenger Willister had left their conference less than half an hour before and the impact of his visit was still settling in. They all decided it was fortunate that there were few others in the Officers' Mess, given their new orders.

"What did you think of Fayrborn?" asked Group Line Chief Goriz, toying with her spoon, coming to the heart of the trouble.

"I think he needs more rest than a week or two on a *Semper*. I think he's up to something. And I don't think he's in any condition to go into combat." Group Line Chief Sventur's face was cool and her eyes remote, but her fingers moved restlessly over the surface of the table.

"No, he's not," Group Line Chief Goriz agreed. "And we'd better be prepared to deal with that."

"Yes," said Sventur.

Group Line Chief Apanali came up to the two women. "Is there room for me?"

Group Line Chief Goriz made a place for him. "We're worried about Fayrborn," she said without prefacing her remarks with disclaimers.

"We don't think he's in any condition to go into combat," said Group Line Chief Sventur.

"That's fairly obvious," said Group Line Chief Apanali. "Even that sperk from The Hub must have noticed it."

"I've put memos in with the others"—by which

Goriz meant the other two Group Line Chiefs—
"asking for a meeting before we leave the *Semper Rigel*. I don't know if they'll come."

"Let's hope they do," said Sventur. "If we have to fight, we need to be prepared." She tasted her xoclat, finding it still too hot. "The state Fayrborn's in, he—"

"He's been this way for months," said Apanali. "And he isn't getting any better. Two weeks ago he drew his tazer on Communications Leader Gaikhu: he threatened to shoot her. The Mromrosi stopped it from happening. Gaikhu agreed not to report it."

"He's taken to carrying a stealth saber, with the laser fittings in addition to the blade," said Sventur. "I saw him with it a few days ago. He was cleaning the blade and talking to it. He's in bad shape, and that's bad for all of us." She said nothing of the threat Fayrborn had made to her then—that he would gut and skin her if she complained to the Fleet Commodore about his behavior.

"He'll make it worse for us," said Goriz. "After what happened on Buttress, I'm worried about him."

"Small wonder," said Sventur. "Any officer who would want to wipe out a settlement because his translator wasn't working and so he decided that they were speaking against him . . . He was ready to give the order." She shook her head slowly. "We're lucky it didn't turn nasty."

"Because you wouldn't let it, Sventur," interjected Apanali. "You kept him from breaking down."

"I was nearest. We all knew what was going on," Sventur said.

"And this time we have real trouble," said Goriz, her bright green eyes shining.

It happened very quickly. A tall young man in a Petit Harrier uniform with The Hub colors on his sleeve badges appeared in the doorway, moving fast. His stride was long—he could be running—and his platen was in disarray. There was blood and bruises on the side of his face and his eyes, grotesquely swollen in purple abrasions, did not focus well. None of the three Group Line Chiefs could say for certain that this was actually Group Chief Willister, but they could not be sure that it was not.

"The Emerging Planet Fairness Court. Lontano . . . subterfuge. The Grands . . ." The young officer lurched and blood sprayed into the room from the disruptor blast to his back. He dropped into a heap, unable even to twitch.

Sventur was already on her feet and calling for a Bunter when a squad of five Grands in Guard tunics came into the room, nodded efficiently but uninformatively to the others before tucking the body into a blue-and-white Graves' Registration sack.

"Wait a minute—" Sventur began as she rose.

"No time," said one of the Grands as he and the others hastened away.

"What in all the pogging—" began Line Commander Apanali.

Group Line Chief Goriz was on her feet, already hurrying into the corridor, her officer's patch on full so there would be no mistaking her rank or intent.

The other two were right on her heels.

But the hall was empty. The nearest intersections were some distance in both directions. There was no sign of the dead body and not one breathing Grand Harrier anywhere in sight.

"Zamlots," whispered Sventur. "Where did they go?" She asked the question for the other two. "Well?"

"This is very bad," said Group Line Chief Apanali as he started back toward the Mess. He stopped at the half-open door. "Do you wish to . . . go elsewhere?"

"Perhaps it would be better just to walk," suggested Group Line Chief Goriz. She realized her hands were unsteady, and if they walked, she would not give it away.

"I think that's best," said Apanali.

"Yeah." Sventur made an effort to return to what they had been saying before Willister—if it was Willister—was murdered in front of them. "Once we leave this *Semper*, we're under Fayrborn. We'll be answerable to Fayrborn. This time Fayrborn could get us all killed, and start an inter-species war besides." She pressed her lower lip with her teeth. "Pogger all, anyway."

"Ahmeen," said Apanali, who was devout.

Goriz made a gesture of resignation. "What are we going to do? They've given us cross-coded written orders, hand-delivered. We can't get out of it. It's registered in our brains. If we fail, we fry our synapses at the least."

"Then we have to stop Fayrborn *and* the war," said Sventur as if it were the simplest thing imaginable.

"We can stop a war," said Apanali as if there

were no trick to it. "Fayrborn might be another matter. I don't know what we're going to do about him."

"So might the Grands," added Goriz, "be another matter."

"Yeah, the Grands," Sventur echoed glumly.

Charge Lomat Pallisenne was waiting in Line Commander Fayrborn's quarters, his Grand level three dress uniform impeccable. The very ancient Suomish skinning knife he held glistened as much as the braid on his epaulets. "Good evening, Line Commander," he said at his most urbane.

Line Commander Fayrborn stood very still. "Why are you here?" he asked without returning the greeting. He wanted to pull the stealth saber from its hidden scabbard just to show Pallisenne that he, too, appreciated edged weapons.

"To discuss a few things with you. I want to assure myself of your attention," he added, holding up the knife.

"You have it," said Fayrborn, thinking that he ought to be the Grand Charge instead of that Gascoygnai.

"You're the Fleet Commodore's errand boy, aren't you?" He sneered, relishing his contempt.

"Most Secret," said Fayrborn, which was all he could say.

"Too bad," said Charge Pallisenne. "The Marshall-in-Chief wants to know what's up. You're the only one who can tell us. And you haven't been filing your reports as promised."

"I can't, can I? Not with a Most Secret lock

on," said Fayrborn, doing his best to conceal the fear that gripped him.

"There are ways to override a Most Secret lock," said Pallisenne, his grin without a trace of humor.

Now Fayrborn was terrified. He knew, just as every Harrier did, that there were ways to open a Most Secret mental lock, ways that left the mind stripped of memories and logic. His hands were shaking so badly that he shoved them into his hip pockets. "I'm on orders. If I don't command this mission, the mission doesn't leave. You won't gain much."

Pallisenne's expression did not change. "The Marshall-in-Chief of the Grands wants you to know that your transfer might be processed after the mission. Your record will still be clean if you leave soon. We've already made an attempt to . . . find out more, about a quarter of an hour ago. The young officer probably regretted his obduracy at the end. He was not capable of listening to reason. But that's up to you."

There was nothing Fayrborn could say without humiliating himself more than he was already. He tried to maintain his dignity, and wished he had a Kleestick, or his stealth saber in his hands.

"You want that transfer, don't you?" Pallisenne mocked Fayrborn with his question. "The Magnicate Alliance exists because the Grand Harriers protect it, not because the Petits police minor planetary disputes. The Grands are the only ones dealing with the big picture. You do want to be a Grand?"

Fayrborn wanted to be a Grand more than

anything. It had been galling to accept his commission in the Petits, and to have his requests for transfer consistently ignored or refused. To have this opportunity was so tantalizing. "I want to be a Grand."

"Then act like one. Take your orders from the Grands, not from the Petits. Not even from the Fleet Commodore of all the Harriers. We have to know where your loyalties lie. We have to know you're with the Grands. Otherwise upstarts like that Haakogard will get position and importance. Do you want that?" He toyed with his knife. "If there is any hint of betrayal, if you have any idea of playing a double game, I promise you that this"—he lifted the blade toward Fayrborn's throat—"will end up in your liver."

"You don't need to do that," said Fayrborn, swallowing hard.

"I hope that's true." Pallisenne made a circuit of the room. "When you reach Lontano, take your orders from the Grand Flotilla Master. No more of this accommodation to the Petits. You owe us, Fayrborn."

"All right," said Fayrborn, trying to match Pallisenne's cool authority. "And if there are questions from The Hub?"

"Make sure there aren't," said Pallisenne. "You Petits aren't going to get mixed up in that skirmish. This time you're going to have to let the Grands handle it."

"I'll do my part," said Line Commander Fayrborn, already starting to think of himself as Flotilla Master Fayrborn, the rank that ought to have been his from the first.

"Keep in mind the stakes we're playing for, Fayrborn. If we handle it just right, we can break the back of the Emerging Planet Fairness Court. No more Mromrosii keeping an eye on us, no more need to follow the rules those six alien races have set down for us. Bonock! Doesn't it make you sick to see those unhuman things lord it over us? Space is for humanity, for The Hub and the Magnicate Alliance, and we shouldn't need the permission of huge predatory insects"— by which he meant the sagacious and gentle Wammgalloz—"or gaseous will-o'-the-wisps"—by which he meant the preternaturally sensitive Cyi—"or muscular starfish"—by which he meant the Ghethept—" or idiotic clown wigs"—by which he meant the Mromrosio—"or the rest of them to be out here."

Charge Pallisenne's outburst so completely matched Line Commander Fayrborn's innermost convictions that he could hardly bring himself to speak. "If I can contribute anything . . . *anything* at all . . ."

"Do your part in this and you'll share our glory," Pallisenne promised. "One more thing. Just a word of caution. In case you think you can change your mind out there. One of your officers is working for us. And he will kill you if you don't do your job." He chuckled at the shock Fayrborn was unable to conceal.

"One of my officers?" Fayrborn repeated dumbly. "On my ship or in the mission?"

Charge Pallisenne only laughed.

The Senior Bunters were assembled on the

staging deck, each with its own inventory for its ship. The Senior Bunter of the *Suidotal* was still attached to the ship's servo-system, finishing the last stages of loading and stowing. It had reported finding the body of Maintenance Supervisor Barr Zeitmein to Security and was still waiting to turn the body over to someone in authority.

At six-thirty, Group Line Chief Apanali presented himself at the staging deck, his uniform splendidly neat, the red horse-head tag of the Petit Harriers on his collar, shining, his ship's flashes glistening red-and-silver. He paled when informed of the dead Maintenance Supervisor. "When did he die?"

"An hour ago, more or less," said the Senior Bunter for the *Yamapunkt*. "His spinal cord was cut and scrambled with a laser weapon of some kind."

"A stealth weapon?" asked Group Line Chief Apanali, making the guess he wanted to be wrong.

"It is most likely so," said the Senior Bunter. "I surmise that someone was waiting for him when he came on duty, which would have been eighty Earth Standard minutes ago."

The other Senior Bunters hummed in agreement.

"Well, keep it quiet," he ordered as he gave it his consideration. "The fewer of us know about it, the better. We can't make this mission more risky than it already is."

The Senior Bunters signaled their acceptance of the order, and posted one of their number to stand guard over the body until Security claimed it.

"You're informed about this mission? You're aware of what's happened?" Group Line Chief Apanali asked his Senior Bunter, trying to do his work properly; the dead Maintenance Supervisor remained in his thoughts like a stubborn pebble in his shoe.

"There are certain orders in the cybernetic system, yes. Very new and unexpected." The Senior Bunter made a clicking sound. "We are ordered to go to Lontano without formal mandate."

"That's the basics," said Group Line Chief Apanali. He was tired, the back of his head feeling not-quite-awake. He had taken two stimulants while he showered but neither had kicked in yet, and with the body to consider he did not think he could concentrate properly. "I need a full report of weapons, fuel and ammunition," he said to the Senior Bunter. "For all the ships."

"Of course," said his Senior Bunter, examining the clips attached to him. "We can present you with complete data in three Earth Standard minutes."

"Quite satisfactory," said Group Line Chief Apanali, glancing around as he heard the whiffling sound of a Mromrosi.

He liked to think that the mound of curly orange hair with the single bright green eye mounted atop was his Mromrosi, the one the Emerging Planet Fairness Court had assigned to his ship, and no other. He fancied he could recognize that one. But, in fact, there was no way humans had found to tell one Mromrosi from another, and this might be his or one of the other five with their mission. This one bounded up to Group Line Chief Apanali on all eight of his short little legs, apparently expressing enthusiasm about their departure; he stood about as high as Group Line Chief Apanali's shoulder, which was tall for a Mromrosi. Unless he was stretching, in which case it might mean little or nothing.

"There is misfortune at Lontano. It is appropriate that we depart at once." He favored Group Line Chief Apanali with a long, penetrating, green stare.

"We depart very shortly. We're not quite ready yet," said Group Line Chief Apanali.

"It is wise to maintain readiness," declared the Mromrosi, his cascade of curls turning from orange to chrome yellow.

"We've done that," said Group Line Chief Apanali, doing his best to be reasonable. There was no telling what the Mromrosi might intend by this observation.

"But one must always remember that there is surprise, both pleasant and unpleasant," the Mromrosi declared, and headed for the *Ikemoos*. So it *was* his Mromrosi; Group Line Chief Apanali felt very proud of himself.

While he was watching the Senior Bunters process all their inventories and print out a written record for him, Group Line Chief saw Communications Leader Gara Gaikhu come sauntering into the staging deck. Her green-and-purple flashes identified her as one of the *Yamapunkt*'s officers.

"Morning," said Communications Leader Gaikhu, her eyes flicking over Group Line Chief

Apanali in cool evaluation. There were rumors about her and a number of Petit Harrier officers that Apanali had always thought exaggerated, but seeing her this way, he wondered. She did not smile at him, but neither did she leave him standing by himself.

"Morning," said Group Line Chief Apanali. "Where's everyone else?"

"Most of them are having a bite to eat, to wake up." She looked toward the *Yamapunkt*. "His nibs in yet?"

"If you mean Line Commander Fayrborn, no he isn't," said Group Line Chief Apanali, his manner becoming stiff. He decided to say nothing about the dead Maintenance Supervisor. "No one has arrived on board that I know of."

"Lighten up, GLC. I don't mean anything against you. We've got a LC who's scared of shadows and orders that head us right into trouble. We're going on a chancey mission. What do you expect me to do? Dance?" She was a very beautiful woman if your taste ran toward leggy, small-busted brunettes. She wore her Class Six standard uniform with distinction and carried herself with an air.

"Line Commander Fayrborn accepted our orders," said Group Line Chief Apanali formally. "We're all bound by our oaths to the Petit Harriers and The Twelve."

"Right," said Communications Leader Gaikhu. "And we have to follow Fayrborn. Great." She started toward her ship and paused to check in with the Senior Bunter. Before she went up the gangway, she looked over at Group Line Chief

Apanali. "I hope we might have a drink after it's over. If you Kousrauni socialize with Kiriopolites."

"Persia and Greece stopped fighting a long time ago," said Group Line Chief Apanali, recalling the legends that had made his childhood so fascinating. "Even in Old Earth terms."

Communications Leader Gaikhu chuckled as she went aboard.

"What was that all about?" asked Protocol Officer Group Leader Jarez gos Mecur of the *Reiwald*, who had left Yerba Buena more than fifteen years before and showed no desire to return, no matter how lovely the planet. He had a look of permanent disbelief about him, which was often the case with Protocol Officers, who were usually expert spies as well as diplomats. He stared at the skimmers and gave a single, pained sigh. "I suppose we have to follow orders. Pity. How much longer before we leave? Twenty minutes?"

"Nothing more," said the Senior Bunter of the *Reiwald*. "You should go aboard, sir."

"Possibly, possibly," said Protocol Officer Group Leader gos Mecur. "But I think I'll have one last look at the game room before I leave." He turned on his heel and almost bumped into Executive Officer Jaan Duykster from Neue Neue Amsterdam, of the *Daichirucken*. "Morning," he said, exchanging the most minimal salutes.

"And to you," said Executive Officer Duykster. He looked over at the Senior Bunter for the *Daichirucken*, his flash of the ship's gold-and-black colors identifying him among the other Senior Bunters. "Who's aboard?"

"You're the first, sir," said the Senior Bunter. "Group Line Chief Sventur has notified me that she is on the way. A most unusual turn of events. And coming at a . . . an awkward time."

"Yes," agreed Executive Officer Duykster. "Morale isn't what it should be, understandably. But that is—In any case. Let's hope that it doesn't turn out—" He broke off as he went toward the gangway.

"There is something you should be aware of," the Senior Bunter of his ship said, detaining him. "It will have to be kept confidential for a short while."

"What will?" Executive Officer Duykster asked, becoming apprehensive at the withdrawn tone of the Senior Bunter.

"There has been a . . . misfortune." The Senior Bunter was about to go on when Executive Officer Duykster tried to cut it short.

"You mean Willister? Yes, that was shocking. But we have a duty to do." He made no attempt to hide his nervousness but neither did he display it.

"Sadly, there is another . . . event you ought to be aware of," said his Senior Bunter, and indicated where the Maintenance Supervisor was being guarded. "He died little more than an hour ago."

"An accident?" Duykster asked, hoping against the certainty he felt.

"Unfortunately, it would appear he was murdered," said the Senior Bunter.

"Great," muttered Duykster. "Two in one night, and we're not underway yet."

"Most certainly, sir," the Senior Bunter agreed. It swiveled its upper body and made a last survey of the area, then followed Executive Officer Duykster up the gangway and into the Glavus-class skimmer.

The Senior Bunter of the *Ikemoos*—flashes red-and-silver—lingered by the gangway, still showing as much apprehension as a machine could: three little lights blinking on its shoulder. At its base the body of Maintenance Supervisor Zeitmein continued to cool.

"Trouble?" asked Group Line Chief Praechee of the *Sakibuckt*, preparing to go aboard his ship. "Is something wrong?"

He was informed of the dead Maintenance Supervisor, which made him swear colorfully for two minutes. "Any idea who did it?"

"No, Group Line Chief, we have no idea," said the Senior Bunter.

"Where was Fayrborn when this man was killed, does anyone know?" he asked, directing his question to no one in particular.

"His location is not accounted for," said the Senior Bunter guarding the body.

"I see," said Group Line Chief Praechee, then deliberately changed the subject. "Are we ready to depart?"

"I don't know," said the Senior Bunter, a phrase that was rarely heard from Bunters. "I can find no malfunction, try as I may, but—"

"Check it out again," Group Line Chief Praechee recommended. "If you were human we'd say you have a hunch. I pay attention to hunches, myself."

"It isn't a very specific way of doing things," the Bunter complained, but accepted the recommendation. "But I will run through the circuits once again. In case."

"That is very wise. And get Security here, will you? They should have arrived by now."

"We have issued a third signal," said his Senior Bunter.

"Good show," said Group Line Chief Praechee, pausing on the gangway as he heard the cheerful call of his Communications Officer.

"We're coming. I saw Brere back there along the corridor, and Marillo was right behind him. Some of the others are finishing breakfast." He hurried up the gangway. "We're going to have to move some if we plan to lift off at seven. By the look of us, the ships aren't ready yet."

Group Line Chief Praechee made a gesture of resignation. "You know how things are when The Hub starts issuing orders." He did not mention the murdered man.

Protocol Officer Nikli Doninov was from Vladimir and had been to The Hub once in his life. He nodded sagely as if he shared special knowledge, and went on into the ship.

The mission was away by seven-fifteen, which most of the Group Line Chiefs considered a spectacular accomplishment which could only be credited to Leatris Sventur, who kept them all moving, reminding them it was her home planet under attack.

Security had yet to claim the body of Maintenance Supervisor Zeitmein when the mission cast off.

"Course to Lontano," Line Commander Fayrborn ordered his Navigator, checking the surveills as the *Semper Rigel* vanished behind them in the vast field of stars.

"Laid in and ready," said the Navigator. "Other ships in the mission already coordinated."

Although this was entirely correct and would ordinarily win the Navigator a word of praise for efficiency, Line Commander Fayrborn was already at the limit of his endurance. "Taking a lot on yourself, aren't you? I suppose you didn't think it necessary to ask me anything?"

"No," said his Navigator, a quick-thinking woman from Mere Philomene in her thirties who had been doing her job for more than ten years. "And neither do you," she added without apology. "You told me to handle it, Line Commander. Did you forget?"

In fact, Line Commander Fayrborn had forgotten, but would not admit as much to her. "Still, you ought to have received my order." He stood a little straighter. "Keep on with it. Confirm formation of the rest of the mission."

"Check the surveills, why don't you?" Navigator Panmix asked before reading out all the information displayed at her station. "*Reiwald* on point, *Sakibuckt* tailing. *Suidotal*, *Daichirucken* and *Ikemoos* in formation immediately behind and four points below."

"Satisfactory," said Line Commander Fayrborn. He turned around toward his ship's Mromrosi and glowered at the alien. "For your report."

"We are not required to submit reports of that nature," said the Mromrosi as if he were unaware of the Line Commander's attitude. "However, I will note your efficiency, if that is so important to you."

"Fool," Line Commander Fayrborn muttered, and did not notice how his bridge officers exchanged uneasy glances. "Prepare for superlight," he ordered briskly as if trying to create a better impression on his officers.

"Prepared," said his Executive Officer Boro Omerrik, recently transferred in from duty on a Broadsword. He was from Buttress and had made the Harriers his home as many other Buttrines had.

"Other mission ships prepared," Communications Leader Gara Gaikhu relayed as the other five signaled readiness.

"Superlight," said Line Commander Fayrborn, feeling master for the situation, if only for a few seconds. He held his hands tightly clasped behind his back to keep them from shaking. What had happened to that messenger? When he asked for a complete log of departure reports as they left, there had been no indication at all that Group Chief Willister had ever arrived on the *Semper Rigel* let alone ever left it. If only, he thought bitterly, his mother had not married a metals-dealer, he might have been eligible for the Grands instead of being stuck forever in the Petits. He had the right talents for the Grands. He *belonged* in the Grands. His manners were excellent, he was adept at politics and he loved the convoluted games of diplomacy. But thanks to his mother's caprice and the avarice of her family, the nearest he would ever get—without patronage—was the upper ranks of the Petits, which now seemed more remote to him than the most distant radio-galaxy known. How he kept from screaming at the injustice of it, he could not imagine.

"How bad is it on your ship?" The message came very late at night, when only a few crucial stations were manned. Leatris Sventur pushed herself onto her elbow and signaled her Bunter to remain inactive.

"Aside from worries about Fayrborn, not too bad. There's nothing from the *Semper Rigel* on the murders. We're hoping for word about Lontano." She kept her voice low.

"Yeah. We're getting restive over here," said Group Line Chief Hsuin. "There aren't any Lontaniani on the *Suidotal*, but we're nervous anyway. I'm sorry it's rough on you."

"Thanks," said Group Line Chief Sventur. She was awake enough to be curious about the call. "Why? What's the matter?"

"Fayrborn's the matter," said Group Line Chief Hsuin bluntly. "We could be going into combat, and we've got him in charge. You know his condition. He isn't getting any better. He's been fondling that stealth saber of his as if it was part of his anatomy. We might as well surrender now and save equipment and lives."

"I can understand why you feel that way," said Group Line Chief Sventur reluctantly. "I feel a little that way myself."

"No kidding," said Hsuin. "There are over forty personnel on this ship, not to mention Bunters and our Mromrosi. I'm responsible for them. I don't like having someone like Fayrborn issuing the orders when I might have to answer for them."

"It bothers me, too," Sventur admitted. "It doesn't do any good to speculate, but I can't stop. I've got family on Lontano, and I don't know what's happened to them. If we have to rely on Fayrborn to help them . . ." She realized that Hsuin could not see her shrug, but she shrugged anyway.

"I've been talking to the others. To be prepared."

Sventur puckered her lips. "What did you say?"

"Prepared. I said prepared." This admission was hurried. "So far everyone's feeling about the same."

The enormity of that statement shocked Sventur, and she needed a second or two to digest what she had been told. "You're telling me that you're prepared to mutiny?"

"We're prepared to stay alive and try to do something about the planet. We've got orders from the Fleet Commodore, with Most Secret locks, and Fayrborn's not following them, and that worries me," Hsuin corrected. "With Fayrborn in charge, we could be stuck in orbit until the next nova event, or he might decide to take on every Bombard in the Grand fleet, and that would be that."

"The Mromrosii wouldn't permit either of those things, would they?" Sventur asked. "They've stopped other mutinies."

"If Fayrborn doesn't kill them first, I guess they might. But I don't want to have to depend on six fuzzy aliens to keep Fayrborn sane. It's bad enough being under Most Secret orders, and having Fayrborn in charge . . . well—"

Sventur considered this and nodded. "All right. For the sake of argument, let's pretend I agree; we could be goats."

Hsuin was at once reticent. "Oh, no. No hedging. It's too risky for all of us. I need you to give your word that you will not betray us. Fayrborn would have us all killed for insubordination, and who knows what would happen at Lontano."

She leaned her head back. "I can't promise to support you, but I won't give you away. You have my word: I'll keep your confidence," she said at last, realizing that she was more apprehensive about Fayrborn than she had let herself know. "If that's good enough?"

"Fine," said Hsuin, clearly relieved. "That's all we ask. Here's what we've agreed upon: when we reach Lontano, if Fayrborn is behaving then as he is now, Group Line Chief Goriz will take charge; she's next in command. She'll handle everything, and put Executive Officer Omerrik in charge of the *Yamapunkt*. I don't know what we'll do about Fayrborn, but we won't confine him unless it's absolutely necessary. I don't think it's going to be so important; no one will listen to him anyway, once we make the change, and it's not as if he'll have anywhere to go. If he's disarmed, he won't be any danger. We'll program the Senior Bunter to look after him, as well as his own Bunter."

"And if we have casualties?" Sventur asked. "We'll need those Bunters. Who's going to take care of the wounded?"

"There are enough Bunters without those two,"

said Hsuin, unwilling to debate the matter. "The usual battle requirements are one Bunter to five wounded."

"But they monitor everything—fuel, ammunition, damage—if things get out of hand, the Bunters'll be spread pretty pogging thin." Sventur waited for an answer.

"We'll manage, believe me," Hsuin assured her.

"If you think so," Sventur said, feeling doubtful.

"Goriz and Praechee are agreed that this would be the best solution for the time being, since we don't know what we're up against." Hsuin paused. "Apanali thinks it would be better if we made certain he couldn't do anything."

"Confine him to quarters during conflict?" Sventur suggested. "That won't look good if the Marshall-in-Chief investigates."

"No, it wouldn't," said Hsuin. "But getting wiped out because of Fayrborn would look .look worse."

"It would," said Sventur, thinking of her relatives; she could only imagine what they could be going through, and her imagination had been horribly overactive.

"Will you help us?" Hsuin sounded anxious.

"If I can," said Sventur. "I won't get in your way, in any case. And I won't say anything. But I'm putting Lontano ahead of all other considerations. If having Fayrborn around will help my home planet, then he pogging well better be on the bridge. If he bollicks, then lock him up." She was startled at the depth of her emotion, but relaxed as much as she could. "Keep me informed."

"We make dropout tomorrow afternoon," Hsuin

reminded her. "We might not have many more chances to talk."

"Leave a coded confidential message with my Bunter. It'll be secure." She began to feel restless, shifting her position in bed as if she were going to get up. "I'll put in a personal code to your voiceprint. Look, I don't want to get caught in a political game with the Grands. I want to get those invaders off Lontano. I want to make sure the planet's safe. That's my job and it's what I'm going to do."

"That's what we want to do," Hsuin promised her.

She paused, then spoke about something that had been bothering her since their mission began. "If it was Willister who got killed back at *Semper Rigel*, did he communicate with The Hub before he died? It's possible, isn't it, that we're going to look like mutineers in any case? Because there's no record of our orders being delivered?"

Hsuin coughed gently. "It's possible," he allowed.

"So we could be held accountable for anything that happens, and tried as mutineers?"

"There are records, Sventur. Back at the *Semper Rigel*, there are Most Secret locks on files, and everything we need is there." Hsuin said it with heavy emphasis, as if he himself did not quite believe it.

"But something could happen, couldn't it? Those Most Secret files disappear from time to time, don't they?" She cleared her throat once more. "Don't they?"

There was one other thing Hsuin wanted her to know. "According to Communications Leader Gaikhu on the *Yamapunkt*, there've been two zaps to Fayrborn from the Grands."

"The Grands?" Sventur repeated in an outraged whisper. "Why would the Grands be sending zaps to this mission? What do the Grands want with Fayrborn? Or Lontano? Or us?"

"We don't know. Gaikhu said she'd try to find out, but she's not making any promises. It's going to get complicated," said Hsuin.

"And we dropout tomorrow afternoon," said Leatris Sventur, feeling very vulnerable.

"Talk to you later," said Hsuin, and coded out.

Six Earth Standard days from the *Semper Rigel* and they dropped out of their superdrive into speeds reckoned in sub-light units. They were approaching Lontano's system and they did not want to get too close to the planet without making a thorough check on it. The zaps that had followed them with coded messages had warned them that the situation had deteriorated, and that information was sketchy at best. The three mission officers from Lontano did their best to ignore that news.

"So what do you think the Grands are doing here?" Group Line Chief Goriz asked Line Commander Fayrborn as they both spotted the four Grand Harrier Petards hanging in orbit around Lontano.

"Protecting the interests of the Magnicate Alliance," said Line Commander Fayrborn, trying to conceal the envy that filled him. His longing to be with the Grands was so great it was almost like a physical weight pressing on him.

"I thought that's what we're here to do," said Group Line Chief Goriz. "Have you signaled them?"

"Naturally," said Line Commander Fayrborn.

Group Line Chief Goriz cursed silently, knowing that her distress was shared by the other Group Line Chiefs. "And has there been any contact?"

"The Charge of the mission informed me that a dispatch will be ready soon," said Line Commander Fayrborn, grateful that he would not have to make any immediate decisions.

"And what about Lontano? Have you notified Capacitta that we've arrived?" Group Line Chief Goriz was growing impatient.

"The Grands have said we're to maintain silence until they provide us a release." It was lovely to have the authority of the Grands, even vicariously.

"We aren't under orders from the Grands," said Group Line Chief Apanali. "We're under specific order from the Fleet Commodore; with provisos for no superseding. You probably shouldn't have informed the Grands we'd arrived. You weren't instructed to."

Fayrborn was shocked at the notion. "That's ridiculous. Their surveills would pick us up, no matter what. We're all Harriers and we all answer to the same Fleet Commodore, Grands and Petits alike." That last was a nice touch, he decided. He watched the faces of his Group Line Chiefs on the surveills and gnawed his lip. "Listen. If we didn't notify them of our arrival, the Grands could consider us potential enemies and commandeer our ships. You all know that."

"Not if we're designated a mission of the Fleet Commodore," said Group Line Chief Sventur. "You know as well as I do, Line Commander, that we're not answerable to the Grands, not those, not any of them." Now that she saw her home planet looming in her surveills, she longed for contact with the surface, to find out how great the damage was, and how many of her family were caught up in the hostilities.

"What the Fleet Commodore says at The Hub is fine. He doesn't have to face aliens attacking this remote place. All he has to do is send his aides with orders." Fayrborn knew how petulant that sounded, but he was not about to apologize or explain.

"You should have waited for them to contact you," said Fayrborn's own Protocol Officer, which infuriated the Line Commander, though the Protocol Officer was a Lontaniano and understandably upset.

"I know my duty, Mister!" Line Commander Fayrborn burst out, and quieted himself as quickly as possible. "If you were in my position—"

"—I would have kept silent; that's what the book requires," said Protocol Officer Diam Bontorn, his face set in condemnation.

Behind Line Commander Fayrborn, Navigator Korliss Panmix made a face and shook her head to show her frustration. "Where do you want the formation to hold, Line Commander?" she asked, although Gilyard Fayrborn was the last person she trusted to decide about that.

"Wait until I hear from the Flotilla Master on the lead Petard," said Line Commander Fayrborn.

"I don't think that's a very wise idea, sir," said Executive Officer Omerrik. "It's my duty to make note of decisions that appear to be contrary to the purpose of our mission, and from where I sit—"

He got no further. "You are relieved, Mister Omerrik," said Line Commander Fayrborn. "Report to your quarters and remain there until your Bunter informs you that—"

The Mromrosi had been watching this without interruption, his mass of curls changing from muted yellow to candy-cane pink to a muddy russet; his single green eye shone brightly. "It is my impression that your Executive Officer is in the right, Line Commander," he said suddenly.

Executive Officer Omerrik was almost off the bridge when he heard this, and stopped. "Thank you," he told the alien.

"There is no need for thanks, Executive Officer," the Mromrosi said calmly. "This is nothing more than an unfortunate misunderstanding. It is not correct for you to be off the bridge at this time. Therefore I think it might be best if we all review the terms of the sealed orders." His color was now a startling thallo green.

"Why do you say that?" demanded Line Commander Fayrborn. "You shouldn't know about those orders."

The Mromrosi bounced toward him on his eight little legs. "We of the Emerging Planet

Fairness Court have access to all pertinent documents and records," he said. "Therefore, I recommend you allow the review, Line Commander."

Line Commander Fayrborn nearly balked; he did not want to listen to anything the Mromrosi had to say, and he wanted Executive Officer Omerrik out of there. Yet he knew he was obliged to pay attention to the Mromrosi. Every Harrier ship had to answer to its Mromrosi. "All right," he growled. "We'll review, as soon as we hear from the Petard."

"Now would be more appropriate," said the Mromrosi. "Your rank is equal to that of the Flotilla Master. You need not acquiesce to his orders."

"I said we would wait for word from the first Petard." He looked like an obstinate child, his lower lip thrust forward. "I am not going to act without being in accord with the Grands."

"That was not the purpose of your orders, Line Commander," said the Mromrosi. "You were given leave to act *without* the knowledge or consent of the Grands, and I believe the Fleet Commodore had good reasons for issuing such orders."

None of the Group Line Chiefs had anticipated this interjection of the Mromrosi. They all watched with fascination.

"I want you off the bridge," said Line Commander Fayrborn, and paid no attention to the shock this order created among his crew.

"I will comply, of course," said the Mromrosi, "but not because of your order, which does not apply to any member of the Emerging Planet Fairness Court. I will comply because I perceive my presence contributes to your exacerbated responses." He bounced along on his eight stubby legs, his color fluctuating from beige to olive-drab and back again.

"Jhum!" Line Commander Fayrborn would have used a more condemning name for the intrusive and ludicrous alien, but he feared that one of his officers might report his behavior and his lack of respect for the Mromrosi would count against him.

"Line Commander," said Boro Omerrik as he took up his station once again, "for the record, I want to say that I do not support your actions against the Mromrosi. And I am opposed to contacting the Grands because it supersedes the orders we were given. We are answerable only to Fleet Commodore Grizmai. Anything other than strict obedience is contrary to the oath we were required to take."

"Understood," said Line Commander Fayrborn, feeling a bit better now. "Communications Leader Gaikhu, you enter it into the official records, to keep our Buttrine happy. Since he has been elected to continue his work." He put his hands on his hips as he watched the surveills, his attention on the Petards.

The Mromrosi went golden yellow and silent as he departed.

Group Line Chief Leatris Sventur was startled to see the door to her quarters whisk open, and a moment later the single green eye of her ship's Mromrosi appear around it, curls a gorgeous shade of golden-russet. She had not yet fallen asleep and so did not have to jolt herself awake, but she was not completely alert, either. "Yes?" she said, a little surprised that her Bunter had not intercepted the Mromrosi.

"Your Bunter has not malfunctioned, Group Line Chief," said the Mromrosi as he came frolicking toward her. "I have taken the liberty of putting a temporary restraint on it, so that it cannot respond to anything but overt attack, which is not likely to occur. I will restore it to working order when I leave."

Sventur had not been aware that Mromrosii could alter the cyborgs in this way. "Why have you done this?"

"I think it would be advisable for us to talk, Group Line Chief," said the Mromrosi, bustling into Sventur's quarters and closing the door quickly. "I am afraid that I and my associates have agreed that there is excellent reason to anticipate great trouble here. For that reason, I have come to discuss the state of affairs with you and to seek your advice, as well as to speculate on courses open to you now."

Group Line Chief Sventur cocked her head. "Speculate? Why do you say that?"

"Because it is clear to all of us that Line Commander Fayrborn is above his intellectual and emotional capacities to function well and therefore has become a disadvantage to the mission. Doubtless you are aware of this; everyone is." The Mromrosi hopped up onto the end of Sventur's bed and peered down at her with his single benevolent eye.

"To act against him is mutiny," said Group Line Chief Sventur, hoping that the Mromrosi was unaware of the plans the other Group Line Chiefs had in readiness. "Mutiny is a death-penalty offence."

"That is not my assessment, that such an act would be mutiny, that is," said the Mromrosi, turning a soft shade of chestnut. "Nor is it the assessment of my associates. Or, for that matter, your fellow Group Line Chiefs, or so we reckon." He—at least everyone called him he, as they called all Mromrosii he because few humans had sorted out the complicated six-sexed species—positioned himself more comfortably on the foot of Sventur's bed. "We wish to inform you, by which we include all Group Line Chiefs of this mission, that we would regard as favorable any action that removed you from the caprice of your current Line Commander."

"You *want* us to mutiny?" Sventur inquired, thinking she must have misunderstood what the Mromrosi had said. "Assuming it's possible."

"Want is not the issue here. We believe that if this mission is to carry out its orders and serve the purpose for which it is intended, then it must be undertaken without the leadership of Line Commander Fayrborn. Correcting this is not mutiny, but a necessary adjustment. We do not espouse rebellion, but we do not approve disaster by consent, either." The Mromrosi thought about his statement as if reviewing it for error. "I do not see that continuing to act on Line Commander Fayrborn's orders will help in any way to create the desired result."

"Whatever that may be." Sventur was listening very carefully, as if by attention alone she might be able to work out the meaning the Mromrosi was trying to convey. "And you want me to tell the others?"

"Nothing like that," said the Mromrosi, turning a deep blueberry shade. "My associates have undertaken that task."

"You mean, you're all talking to us?" Sventur asked.

"That is essentially correct," said the Mromrosi. "We wish you to be aware of our position as you decide which course to follow. I suspect that you have considered making some effort to avert the most destructive of Line Commander Fayrborn's impulses."

"You are offering to protect us if charges of mutiny are brought against us?" She could not accept what he was telling her. "Would you keep us from freeze-drying?" This was the current execution of choice for mutiny.

"Of course," said the Mromrosi. "The Emerging Planet Fairness Court would not expect you to take the brunt of such a charge, and we would never countenance freeze-drying you."

"Would that make any difference? The Fleet Commodore gave us secret orders. Revealing the orders is also a freeze-drying offence, if the Fleet Commodore wants to be strict about it." She was sitting up now, and she could feel tension gather in her body. Her Bunter would have to massage it away if she were to get any sleep at all.

"The Fleet Commodore would have to accept our ruling in this case, as we would be answerable for your actions." The Mromrosi stretched himself up so that he was about a third again as tall as he usually was. "There are issues here you do not fully comprehend. There are questions that you have not asked because you lack the knowledge to ask them. Therefore it is fitting if you permit the Emerging Planet Fairness Court to advise you."

"If you say so," Sventur told him, having difficulty following the Mromrosi's train of thought.

"When you Group Line Chiefs have your next contact, we Mromrosii will be with you, to aid you in your deliberations. We have useful observations to contribute, you may be certain." He hopped down from the bed and scampered across her quarters back toward the door. "Your Bunter will be in correct working order in less than a minute, Group Line Chief Sventur," he said as he slipped out of the room.

Sventur stared at the place where the Mromrosi had been, wondering if this could have been a particularly realistic nightmare. But she knew she had not dreamed it, and that the Mromrosi's warning was genuine. Her hope to be left out of the conflict between the Group Line Chiefs and the Line Commander vanished. She would have to choose a side, and the only side that was acceptable was the Group Line Chiefs. With a gesture of resignation she got out of bed and started toward the bathroom; a few seconds later her Bunter followed her, fixing its massage units in place.

"Does everyone have an inventory for ordnance?" asked Group Line Chief Apanali.

"According to the latest zap, we're to head down to the surface in two hours."

"Not according to Fayrborn," said Group Line Chief Praechee. "He's said no one is to move until the Grands give the go-ahead. The Flotilla Master still hasn't acknowledged our existence."

"Pog the Grands," said Group Line Chief Hsuin. "If we wait for the Grands, we'll be here for a decade, and we'll catch all the sperk. I say we put Goriz in charge, the way we planned. The Mromrosii are right."

There were guarded nods all around, made huge by the surveills. In the *Sakibuckt*, the ship's Mromrosi turned intense scarlet, then faded to the same shade of taupe the other Mromrosii were.

"So what do we do now?" asked Sventur, fearing for her family on the planet. "There's a communications blackout, probably from the Petards. We can't get through without specific permission, and you know Fayrborn won't ask for it."

"We will make arrangements," said the Mromrosi on the *Ikemoos*. "But be prepared to act in two hours."

"Who's going to tell Fayrborn?" asked Group Line Chief Goriz.

"Let us attend to that as well," suggested the Mromrosi from the *Daichirucken*. "The Grands cannot prevent our use of the communications' systems. No matter what the Basatan'gal have done to isolate the planet, there are installations we can reach." He signaled the Communications Leader, Parker Parkerman from Dataline. "You will operate on our authority. In this situation, the Emerging Planet Fairness Court will prevail. Our assumption of responsibility will be voice-printed in your log."

Parkerman acknowledged this, adding, "I'll leave a file open for you, if there are any additions you wish to make. On voice lock."

"An excellent notion!" The Mromrosi of the *Reiwald* seconded Parkerman's suggestion. "Indeed each ship should have such a file at this time. You have much to do. Your Glavuses are not ready for combat, and that is unwise, for combat is going to be waiting for you on Lontano. You will need to spend some of the little time at your disposal to organize your armorments."

The Mromrosi of the *Yamapunkt* added, "Since conditions on the surface are not yet known, we will have to be prepared for more eventualities than would generally be the case. Care will be necessary, and flexibility."

"Right you are," said Group Line Chief Apanali. "We ought to get to it."

"I haven't spotted any alien ships," Group Line Chief Hsuin remarked. "No beacon in orbit, nothing."

"It is not the way of the Basatan'gal. They land on a planet and do everything they can to cut it off from everywhere else. They keep their ships on the surface, not only to fight with the natives, and provide protection in an alien environment, but to decrease the chance of discovery in random sweeps conducted by the Emerging Planet Fairness Court." The Mromrosi of the *Suidotal* spoke with authority. "I have observed them closely, and I know their history."

"Then the fact that we haven't heard anything—" began Group Line Chief Sventur.

"Means little or nothing; the communications blackout the Grands have instigated may be useless," her ship's Mromrosi confirmed. "That is why the matter of consent from the Grands is of no importance. The Grands have not been able to discover anything that they have reported. If there are Grands on the surface, they are mute until we arrange to correct that."

"So we have to go in blind," said Group Line Chief Sventur. "At least I know Lontano. I grew up in Capacitta."

"And we'll have to rely on you," said Group Line Chief Hsuin.

"Of course," said Group Line Chief Apanali. He scanned his surveill, giving the impression that he was looking the other four Group Line Chiefs directly in the eye. "We'd better get at it. Ordnance first, then readiness teams. We leave orbit in one-hundred-seventeen minutes."

The others concurred, and Group Line Chief Hsuin summed it up for the rest of them. "I sure hope we're doing the right thing."

Line Commander Fayrborn was furious. He goggled at the three Group Line Chiefs confronting him and he spat as he swore at them. "You'll freeze for this, all of you!"

"Possibly," said Group Line Chief Apanali. "But that's better than dying out here, picked off by an enemy on the surface we can't see but can pogging sure see us."

"You don't know that. You're only guessing,"

said Line Commander Fayrborn, giving them some of the contempt he had felt from Charge Pallisenne.

"According to the Mromrosii, it's a sperking good one," said Group Line Chief Praechee. "If you'll be good enough to turn over your weapons and your encyphering planchet?"

"You can't do this," Line Commander Fayrborn said, hanging onto his disruptor. "Stand back."

Group Line Chief Praechee shook his head. "Even you aren't stupid enough to fire a disruptor weapon in a ship this size." He said it as if he were talking to a five-year-old.

"I won't have it," Line Commander Fayrborn announced.

"Begging your pardon, sir, but it's done," said Group Line Chief Goriz. "The Bunters have already logged the change and the reason."

"The Grands won't allow it," said Line Commander Fayrborn, "They've said they're—"

"Protecting you?" suggested Group Line Chief Praechee. "Though you're only related to the Lord Mayor of Dickens on your mother's side? Not good enough."

Gilyard Fayrborn stood straighter. "My transfer is all but approved."

"Where is your record of this transfer?" asked Group Line Chief Goriz. "There is no record of it anywhere on this mission."

"Of course there's not," said Fayrborn with an arrogant toss to his head. "Just as there is no record of the officer in this mission who reports to the Grands." He had the satisfaction of seeing alarm in the other's faces. "Surprised you, didn't I?"

"What are you talking about?" demanded Group Line Chief Praechee.

"A double agent, of course. The Grands told me about it." He glared at them. "With officers like you, what could you expect?"

Group Line Chief Apanali shook his head, exasperated and sympathetic at once. "And you *believed* them? Turn over your weapons, Line Commander. We have to leave orbit in fifteen minutes."

"The Grands will inform The Hub," declared Line Commander Fayrborn, desperation making his voice shrill. "And you'll answer for this. Mutiny! You were insubordinate before, but you're light years beyond that now."

"We realize that," said Group Line Chief Goriz, holding her stunner so that it did not point directly at Line Commander Fayrborn.

"I want it on record that I regard this as a criminal act," said Line Commander Fayrborn, trying to retrieve his dignity. "I intend to file formal charges against all of you, and against any members of your crews who supported you."

"You're kidding yourself, Line Commander," said Group Line Chief Praechee. "You're not in a defensi—"

A hissing sound, so low it had been hardly noticeable, grew suddenly louder. The Group Line Chiefs recognized it a second too late, as the odorless, invisible gas of Line Commander Fayrborn's private security unit at last kicked in full strength.

Five minutes later, when the three Group Line Chiefs came to amid the blare of klaxons, they were met by solicitous Bunters, all as chagrined as machines could be, explaining they did not realize that Line Commander Fayrborn was escaping until he had taken a skiff and headed for the *Mon Droit Cassiopeia*.

"Which is where we believe him to be at this moment," finished the Senior Bunter of the *Yamapunkt*.

"Pogger all," said Group Line Chief Praechee, one hand to his head which felt as if it had been swathed in a mass of thick, painfully hot towels.

"What about the landing?" asked Group Line Chief Goriz, forcing herself to think and hating the labor it took to gather her ideas. What gas had Line Commander Fayrborn been using? "We have the alert on hold," said the Senior Bunter of the *Yamapunkt*. "Executive Officer Omerrik ordered it when the skiff cast off."

Group Line Chief Goriz nodded. "Good."

"Group Line Chief Sventur has already worked out the modulations for cast off in five-minute increments for the next two hours," said the Senior Bunter.

A riot of turquoise-blue curls appeared in the space behind the gathered Bunters, and then a huge green eye. The Mromrosi shoved the cyborgs aside and moved nearer. "The report is accurate," he told them. "You were subjected to fantod gas from Hydeyama. But you will recover now. You did not have the lethal dose, of course."

"Or we'd be dead," said Group Line Chief Apanali sourly. He had made it to a crouch and was slowly getting to his feet, not trusting his legs very much.

"Fantod gas," said Group Line Chief Goriz. "So that's what it was."

"Yes. Line Commander Fayrborn's personal Bunter carried the antidote for him at all times." The Mromrosi faded to periwinkle.

"I wish we'd put him in restraints at once," said Group Line Chief Apanali. "Hindsight. It always works."

"He would have escaped in any case," said the Mromrosi. "And there is nothing you can do at this time that will improve your situation. Therefore it is my recommendation that you proceed with your appointed tasks. Group Line Chief Goriz is in command of the mission now."

Emmelein Goriz had tottered to her feet. "And we're holding the alert?"

"Group Line Chief Sventur handled it all admirably; she has even sent a zap to The Hub explaining the circumstances of your attempt to detain Line Commander Fayrborn, and his . . . apparent defection to the Grands. And a special Most Secret read-only to the Fleet Commodore." The Mromrosi bounced restlessly. "So that it cannot be intercepted."

"We hope," said Group Line Chief Goriz. She was feeling a little steadier now. "All right. We'll resume count to descent in ten minutes. In the mean time, I want you all to try to find out what's going on down on the surface. Tell Communications Leader Vonigal to monitor everything, and I mean everything, he can pick up from Lontano."

The Bunters moved first, locating various link-boxes along the wall to pass on Group Line Chief Goriz's orders.

"You think Fayrborn's going to cause any trouble?" asked Hsuin as he practiced walking.

"I think we'd better assume that he is," she answered. When she tried to turn her head quickly, she had to grab the nearest Bunter to keep from falling over. "Weo! That fantod gas is strong stuff."

"It is wise to be monitored for medical disfunction at your earliest convenience," said the Bunter.

"I'll keep that in mind," said Group Line Chief Goriz, thinking that time might not come until after they lifted off from Lontano.

They chose Seicancel, fifty kilometers north of Capacitta, as their landing place, for their readings had shown that all communications with the capital were blocked. On their second fly-over of three, the small city seemed undisturbed, and its landing field adequate to their needs.

"I have cousins in Seicancel," said Diam Bontorn, the Protocol Officer of the *Yamapunkt*. "I could try to reach them, find out if there's anything they can tell me. They'll trust me. They know I'm one of them."

Since spying was high on the list of Protocol Officers' duties, Executive Officer Boro Omerrik relayed this suggestion to the *Reiwald*, adding to Acting Line Commander Goriz, "It makes more sense to send Bontorn than to send Sventur."

"I need Sventur. She's going to have to scout

for us." Acting Line Commander Goriz was already in battle dress #2, with additional protective gear to screen their short-distance radio transmissions. "Tell Bontorn to get ready. Civilian dress for this area, whatever it's like—he'll know. I want to see him before he leaves. Face to face. I don't want the Grands eavesdropping on us."

"Do you think they're going to interfere?" asked Group Line Chief Hsuin. Of the forty-six human-descent crew members of the *Suidotal*, none came from Lontano. In the mission, Hsuin was one of two Xiaoqing-na. At first he had felt out-of-place and homesick, and thought that The Hub's policy of fully mixed crews was ridiculous. Now, with battle about to begin, he understood why the policy had been adopted, and agreed with it.

"Let's agree that it's likely, and plan for it," she said.

Starting into their third fly-over, Leatris Sventur signaled Emmelein Goriz on her personal beam. "I don't want to make a bad situation worse," she said. "But I have to tell you something. I can't get it out of my head that Fayrborn has someone in the mission still, someone who's . . . who's protecting him. I don't think he made up that claim about another spy. I think it was real."

"I know what you mean," said Goriz.

"I don't want to sound paranoid, but—"

"I know what you mean," Goriz repeated. "It's been eating at me, too. He left . . . too quickly. He didn't cut and run, he set a trap and left."

"Exactly," said Sventur, feeling much relieved.

On the surveills she watched the rolling hills of Tuscareg Province slide away, marked with small hill towns. And something caught her eye. "Wait," she said, switching from her personal beam to her bridge one. "There's something—"

Before she could finish a bright flash filled the screens and the Glavuses rocked in the air. The red-and-silver flashed *Ikemoos* flew to pieces, battering into the sky and breaking into uncountable pieces, tatters of wreckage slamming into the five remaining ships.

Klaxtons whooped, emergency lights went on, and on the five ships, the Navigators and Executive Officers each strove to keep their Glavuses from crashing.

"This is an emergency. This is an emergency," all five Senior Bunters announced to their various ships calmly.

On the *Yamapunkt* the Mromrosi careened into the central surveill and was apparently stunned—at least he became inactive, turned the color of putty, and a fine film came over his single green eye. On the *Sakibuckt* the Mromrosi curled into a tight ball and bounced his way through the turbulence. The other three Mromrosii hunkered down under panel boards on their ships and waited.

As soon as the *Reiwald* ceased to pitch and yaw, Acting Line Commander Goriz picked up her hailer. "Up ten thousand kilometers. Damage report in five minutes."

"Can't do it," said Group Line Chief Hsuin Xanitan. "Our stabilizers are pogged. We've got to get down right now or fall."

"*Suidotal*, land and cover. Do not attempt to meet up with us. When repairs are complete, return to orbit and monitor whatever's going on." It was difficult for Acting Line Commander Goriz to give this order, for she knew she would need every Petit Harrier she could muster to handle this situation—whatever it was.

"We'll do repairs and come after you," said Group Line Chief Hsuin.

"Belay that. Repeat. Belay that. You will return to orbit and monitor. We're going to need documentation, and it'll be your job to get it." She made her voice confident and emphatic, though now that they were ascending rapidly she could hardly hear the transmissions from the crippled *Suidotal*. She had a fleeting thought: the *Suidotal*'s colors were olive-and-orange, providing a little camouflage on the hillside. If one of the ships had to be down, the *Suidotal* would draw the least attention of any of them.

" . . . depending on repa . . . no more than six . . . any . . . snooping. Hsuin ou . . ."

Acting Line Commander Goriz squared her already square Hartzheimer shoulders. "*Sakibuckt*, how bad is your damage?"

"Not too bad, according to the Senior Bunter. What kind of sperk hit us, anyway?" Group Line Chief Praechee sounded more indignant than frightened.

"We'll have full analysis on that in a few minutes," said the Technical Chief of the *Reiwald*, a stalwart young Fils from Mere Philomene. "My own guess is one of those high-impact blasting shells."

"Sounds about right," said Group Line Chief

Sventur grimly. "And if that's what they have down here on the surface . . ."

"That or a disruptor field," suggested the Navigator, who was still wrestling with the helm.

"They're not allowed in this part of the Magnicate Alliance; no disruptor weapons of any kind are allowed on access corridors to the J'zmallir Trade Routes," said Acting Line Commander Goriz.

"They may not be allowed, but that is what destroyed the *Ikemoos*," said the Mromrosi who had turned a neon shade of peach. "Nothing else is destructive in quite that way."

"I would tend to agree," said Group Line Chief Praechee. "I saw them demonstrated last year at the annual Muster. Impressive and terrifying, which is what I suspect was the intention."

"And who has them?" demanded Acting Line Commander Goriz.

"As far as I am aware," said the Mromrosi on the *Reiwald*, "only the Grands have them."

"I mean, of the known human and non-human races," Group Line Chief Praechee specified.

"It is my intention as well. We of the Emerging Planet Fairness Court have records for all space-going species in this part of the galaxy. It is our function." The Mromrosi was abruptly the color of mulberries. "I repeat: in this sector, only the Grands possess such weapons."

Group Line Chief Sventur closed her eyes and turned her face toward the ceiling. "Wonderful. Just pogging wonderful."

"You mean that the Grands are shooting at us," said Group Line Chief Praechee, just to be certain.

"That is what we surmise," said the Mromrosi.

"Group Line Chief," said one of the officers, "There's been a body discovered on the *Reiwald*. Three minutes ago."

"A body?" she echoed.

"With a dagger in his back," said the Senior Bunter of the *Reiwald*. "It is a very old-fashioned weapon. We don't have any clue to follow, for there is no record of any such weapon on board."

"Pog it all," muttered Group Line Chief Sventur.

"Dagger?" echoed her Navigator, Estienne Beaumont of Saint Fou. "And someone's dead?"

"There's a body on the *Reiwald*," said Sventur, her eyes turning hard. "Stabbed."

"Who's dead?" asked Parker Parkerman, like all Dataliners hungry for information first and foremost.

"Who's the victim?" Group Line Chief Sventur asked Group Line Chief Goriz.

"Group Chief Smitz. He's from New Gaia, career Harrier. His field was tracking." Goriz spoke bluntly, not encouraging anyone to volunteer other information.

"Tracking," said Sventur. "Do you think that's important?" Below she could see two ruined bridges. "We'd better head back toward the hills. We're getting too close to Capacitta."

"Right," said Goriz, and gave the order to turn about, adding, "Stay low—fifteen hundred kilometers—until we have a better idea what's going on."

"And make sure the escape kits are handy," added her Executive Officer, Vasilin Nestorenko. "In case we get shot down."

"If they're using disruptor weapons, escape kits won't make a pogging difference," said Communications Leader Gaikhu from the *Yamapunkt*.

"Just in case," said Communications Leader Brere of the *Sakibuckt*. "Keep the escape kits out and handy."

The skimmers had reached the first ridge of the mountains, and they followed it for some distance, taking advantage of the extensive view.

"There's an encampment on the east side of Capacitta that isn't part of the records," said Executive Officer Marillo of the *Sakibuckt*. "What do you Lontaniani think?"

Sventur was the first to answer. "It isn't ours," she said as she called the buildings up on the surveills. "That's not human. Look at those things."

They were strange to look at, leaning at disquieting angles and topped with figures and sculptures that were wholly unrecognizable. The function of the apparent openings of the buildings were not certain, for they appeared too high to be doors and too heavy to be windows. Most of the buildings were lit from within, but the color of the light was hazy, slightly purple in tinge, and it made most human eyes water.

"Better make a record of this, just in case. And relay it to the *Sempers*. We don't want the Grands taking charge of this information," said Goriz, signaling her Communications Leader to get on it.

The Mromrosi on the *Yamapunkt* went a hideous shade of sickly orange. "That is the Bastan'gal; those are their military dwellings."

"What does it mean?" asked Group Line Chief Praechee, watching the same display on his surveills. "Why have they set up their camp right next to the city?"

"It means they control the city, or believe they do," said the Mromrosi on the *Daichirucken*. "That is the way the Bastan'gal behave."

"And they're still in business? Your Fairness Court hasn't stopped them?" Praechee demanded.

"They are already contained, but they have not been abiding by the conditions of our negotiations. Something will have to be done." The Mromrosi turned a deep brown that was almost black.

"Bonock on a pogging stick!" Sventur swore. "How could the Grands let this happen?"

"The Grands are not concerned with Lontano, they are concerned with the Alliance," said the Mromrosi. "If one planet in so many has to be part of the bargain to achieve their ends, then that planet—"

"They're not getting away with it," Sventur declared. "I won't have it." She folded her arms and addressed Group Line Chief Goriz. "We need a conference. At once. If we head back into these hills, we should be able to find a place where we can be safe for an hour or two. We can prepare to deal with the Grands from there."

Goriz heard her out thoughtfully. "I think you're right," she said, "but I'm worried about being on the ground so long. Let's make it forty minutes tops, to lessen the chance of being found in a sweep."

"Right you are," said Sventur, and heard her acceptance echoed by the rest.

"I know a place," said Diam Bontorn suddenly. "It's a sports landing field, for air-yachts. We can get in and out of there quickly."

Sventur agreed at once. "He's right. We can get there in less than half an Earth Standard hour. Forty minutes on the ground and we ought to be ready for anything they decide to throw at us."

"Short of disruptor weapons," ammended Group Line Chief Praechee. "No one's ready for them."

"True," said Goriz, and went silent while Protocol Officer Bontorn gave the coordinates to the rest.

2

It was clearly disruptor fire, and it was coming from more than a dozen installations set all around the sport landing field. As the Glavuses made their first pass over what was the sports landing field, the *Yamapunkt* rocked and shivered under the glancing blow of the disruptor bore.

Now that they had only four ships, they were flying in diamond formation, with the *Reiwald* at the lead, the turquoise-and-bronze flashes charred to a uniform burnt umber. On starboard the *Yamapunkt* bucked and skidded but contrived to keep up with the others without going down. On port was the *Sakibuckt*, in similar condition to the *Yamapunkt*, but in mirror image.

"Hold steady, hold steady," ordered Acting Line Commander Goriz as the Glavuses strove to keep in formation. "Steady."

Then an alarm light went on under the surveill of the *Daichirucken* and a moment later, Group Line Chief Sventur spoke to Goriz on a closed channel. "I don't want to upset you, Acting Line Commander, but we . . . there's a problem here."

"We're all having trouble," said Goriz sharply.

"This is different," said Sventur, and broke off to shout a few terse orders. "There's a body in the biotech section."

"Any injuries?" asked Goriz.

"I said body. Not casualty. This guy was murdered. Like the one found on the *Reiwald*. He had one of those traditional knives stuck up under his sternum." She said it bluntly to make her point.

A last burst of disruptor fire sent all four Glavuses careening through the air. Then they were over the brow of the ridge and temporarily protected.

"Hover," ordered Goriz to all four ships.

"Beg pardon, but wouldn't it be better if—" began Group Line Chief Praechee.

"I said hover, five hundred meters," Goriz said more sternly. "We need to take stock. Right now. This is getting risky."

"What about surveillance?" asked Praechee.

"We need that," said Goriz. "Is your ship steady enough to tend to it?"

"I think so," said Praechee cautiously.

"Do you want to hover, *Yamapunkt*?" asked Goriz.

"Um-hum," agreed Executive Officer Boro Omerrik from the *Yamapunkt*. "We have to check the systems. We're not holding steady." He had already toggled the Senior Bunter to start diagnostics.

"What if they come after us?" demanded Praechee.

"Those disruptors were mounted in the ground. They aren't going to be coming this way any time soon. They're dug in, to keep everyone away from that field. They aren't mobile, for pursuit." Sventur had put the *Daichirucken* in hover and was off the bridge, going toward the biotech facilities, scowling deeply. Behind her the Mromrosi capered, his curls a startling metalic purple. "We've got more immediate things to worry about."

Biotechnician Urthur Mondragon had found the body; he was still greenish. This was his first

114

mission as a Petit Harrier, and he was missing his home on Chalot more than he ever imagined he could.

Group Line Chief Sventur went at once to the corpse. "Has his temperature been checked? Do we know when he was killed?"

"Can't be much more than ten minutes," said the dead man's Bunter that had arrived a minute before. "The blood has not yet coagulated."

She nodded. "Establish the time and the degree of thrust necessary to inflict the wound. Let me know what kind of force we're talking about. I want those figures in half an hour, maximum. And I want to know where everyone was on the ship." She glanced over at Mondragon. "Did he say anything?"

"He was dead," Mondragon replied, speaking with difficulty. "If I'd been a couple minutes earlier, who knows?"

"Yeah," said Sventur, and motioned to the Bunter. "I want this place swept for all evidence. The Senior Bunter will be in charge. Get to work at once. I want a full report before the end of the day, barring other trouble."

"Of course, Group Line Chief," said the Bunter with the usual cyborg calm. "At once."

"And the systems need to be checked. You and the Senior Bunter work around that." She rocked unsteadily as the ship trembled. "I've got to get back to the bridge."

"We will tend to all forensics," the Bunter assured her.

Sventur saluted and left the biotech facilities, the Mromrosi bounding along with her.

"It is troubling, this death," the alien remarked.

"Very troubling. Harriers aren't supposed to kill other Harriers, and that's what happened. I wish I could read it some other way, but—It's what has to have happened, unless you did it. And I can't see how you'd manage to get a dagger into a target that high." She sighed impatiently. "And we're getting dragged into a situation we don't know enough about on top of all this."

"About the murder?" he asked, going a soft mauve.

"No, about Lontano. Lontano is under siege, somehow. And I know in my bones that those sperking Grands waiting up in orbit have something to do about it. They aren't here to protect the planet, that's pog-all obvious. So we can't rely on them. There might be alien invaders—no offence—or there might be a clever ploy on the part of the Grands."

"Maybe it's more than just one siege," suggested the Mromrosi. "It is something to consider."

"Are you telling me that there is a second agenda here?" Sventur stopped still and stared down directly into the Mromrosi's single green eye.

"And possibly a third," said the Mromrosi, faded to lilac. "You have your purpose here, the Grands have theirs."

"Weo. How—" She interrupted herself. "Tell me when we're a bit more secure. I ought to be on the bridge right now."

The Mromrosi accepted this with eager bobbing. "Of course, of course. But a word of advice, Group Line Chief."

"And that is?" she said, continuing up the companionway.

"That is you would do well to send the report of the murder in coded zap, or under seal, directly to Fleet Commodore Grizmai. It would not be wise to make the information too accessible. Do you take my meaning?"

"I think so," said Sventur. "It's dangerous."

"And there are those who might use the information against you rather than to support what you're doing." The Mromrosi brightened to a shade of brilliant pale purple. "It is wise to guard against duplicity."

"That it is," said Sventur as she hurried the rest of the way up the companionway to the bridge.

Goriz was waiting for her report, her larger-than-life image filling the third surveill. "No possible misunderstanding?" she inquired, hope making her tone lighter than it had been.

"Not a chance," said Sventur, dashing them. "Someone murdered the man. I don't think he could have killed himself that way, not without help, and Bunters have a block on suicide assists; he didn't have the information to get around it, not in so short a time."

"No," Goriz agreed morosely. "So someone on your ship and someone on mine is killing people. But who? And why?"

"It would be easier to find out if we weren't in the middle of a war," said Sventur, sighing once. "We have to meet somewhere, and soon. We're too separate, even keeping in contact. The four of us have to prepare. Besides, the contact can be monitored, and that would mean trouble." She sighed and looked toward the ceiling. "I'm putting the *Daichirucken* on silence-block for the next half hour. I suggest you do the same with the rest of the mission. Nothing comes in, nothing goes out."

"Why?" asked Boro Omerrik, the Executive Officer of the *Yamapunkt*.

"I'll tell you when it's over," said Sventur, and turned to her Senior Bunter. "You heard me."

"Your orders will be obeyed except in over-riding emergency." The Senior Bunter began to glow a soft green on its left side, indication of the block being activated.

"Right," said Sventur, then called out: "All officers, in my staging room. Right now. No Bunters." She glanced at the Mromrosi. "You're supposed to be there, aren't you."

The Mromrosi was now a celery green. "Most certainly, Group Line Chief Sventur," he said, and bounded in the direction of the staging room.

The rest were less eager to follow. Group Chief Meahama Godwendo who was in charge of all arms, armor and ammunition, requested permission to be excused so that one of them could remain on the bridge.

"Not granted," said Sventur. "I need you with me. The Bunters can take care of the ship for a short while. They do most of the monitoring in any case. They can warn us if anything goes wrong."

"But they might miss something," protested Group Chief Godwendo.

"So might a human being," snapped Sventur.

"We're in danger of attack," Godwendo persisted.

"From more than one opponent," said Sventur. "And that's why I need you with me in the meeting. Understand?" She was already at the staging room at the rear of the bridge. "Hurry up, all officers."

The staging room had three seals on it, and the recorder worked on circuits unconnected with the rest of the ship, making it virtually impossible to eavesdrop on what was said inside the room. As the officers arrived, they were inspected for weapons and other items, all of which were included in the locked record.

"I don't like this," announced Parker Parkerman as he sat down on Sventur's immediate right. "Secrecy inevitably works against what we're trying to do. The mission requires communication."

Jaan Duykster, the Executive Officer, did not agree. "We don't know why the murders are happening, or who's doing them. If there's a connection, we could make ourselves more vulnerable by maintaining contact."

"I should think that's obvious: whoever is working for Line Commander Fayrborn is responsible," said Parkerman, his attitude growing harsh. "We know that Line Commander Fayrborn has gone over to help the Grands, so—"

"That would mean three or four agents," the Protocol Officer, Zameda Lauy-Rei from Saint Fou, pointed out. "A conspiracy on that scale would probably be conducted in a different manner."

119

"If it is a conspiracy," said Duykster.

"And who are they working for? The Grands? The Bastan'gal? Who?" asked Beaumont. "We haven't enough information to strike back effectively. We're too pogging—"

"We know the Bastan'gal have attacked Lontano, and that's a clear case of aggression," said Duykster. "We can start there and work the rest of it out later."

"You pogging idiot," said Parkerman, looking frightened beneath his bravado. "All the Grands have to do is strand us here and let the Bastan'gal pick us off. They don't have to do anything more aggressive than that."

"What makes you think they aren't doing that right now?" asked Lauy-Rei sweetly, her lean features creased with a sudden, false smile.

Parkerman was prepared to launch into a tirade, but now Group Line Chief Sventur put a stop to it. "There is a killer on at least two of our Glavuses. There is a war on Lontano. And it seems that our Line Commander has joined the Grands in supporting the invaders. We have to prepare ourselves to deal with all these things. First, we must assume that we will receive no help from the Grands, and possibly no help from our own Petits. Second, we must assume that the Bastan'gal invaders are interested in more than raiding; that they are in the process of establishing an outpost—at the very least—on this planet. Third, we have to face the fact that there is a killer loose on two of our ships, possibly more. These three elements may all be related, or they may be coincidental." She slapped the arms of her chair. "All three troubles are real, all of them are immediately dangerous. Do any of you have any suggestions?"

"I can't help but wonder about the Mromrosii," said Navigator Beaumont, the other Saint Founais aboard. "What is their part in this?"

The Mromrosi bounced forward, his curls deepening to a rich raspberry shade. "We are all observers for the Emerging Planet Fairness Court. We do not take any actions unless they have been negotiated prior to the beginning of a mission. In this case, we are merely observing."

"So you say," Duykster whispered.

"Because it is true," declared the Mromrosi. "What reason would any of us have for increasing the danger of your predicament? We are as much a part of your mission as you are. We have as great an interest in its success as you do." He was now lighter and more vibrant, a vivid cerise that seemed too intense for the small staging room.

"But we have only your word on that," said Duykster, more pugnaciously than before. "We have to accept members of the Emerging Planet Fairness Court aboard because you insist on it. For all we know, you aren't policing us, you're taking advantage of our isolation for the purposes of eliminating us."

"We would do that any number of ways, and would not wait until you were at a planet to act. When we have been forced to contain aggressive species, we reach them when they are at superlight speeds, from which they never emerge in any recognizable form." He was now an interesting deep olive color, with a hint of lighter stripes.

"Is that a warning?" asked Lauy-Rei, her temper flaring.

"No, it is offered as useful information," said the Mromrosi, apparently taking no offence at her attitude. "So that you will not confuse our actions with the actions of your enemies."

"Right you are," said Sventur. "So we will turn our attention elsewhere." She rubbed her forehead as if to draw out her thoughts. "I want each one of you to set your Bunters to guard you whenever you are off-duty. I do not want anyone on the ship to be without protection until we find out who the murderer is and why Petits are getting killed. And then I want to do something to save Lontano."

"Makes sense to me," said the Navigator with a hint of a smirk.

Sventur was not amused. "Not just because this is my home, but because we need these distant planets if we're going to work out any means for the Magnicate Alliance to use the J'zmallir Trade Routes. If we let these go—not just Lontano, but Lost Thule and End Zone and the rest of the isolated outposts—then we won't ever have the opportunity to get to the J'zmallir Trade Routes, and that will weaken the Alliance, eventually."

"Most astute," approved the Mromrosi, his single green eye very bright. "It is unfortunate that the Bastan'gal should have decided to ignore the

Emerging Planet Fairness Court restrictions at this time, but it appears you are prepared to deal with the trouble."

"I hope we're able to," said Sventur. "So," she went on to her officers, "first things first. We have to do something about this planet. We have a ship down with a live crew, and they are going to need our help."

"And there is the murderer," said Duykster.

"We'll find out about that, later," said Sventur. "When we know where the trouble comes from."

"From the Grands or the Bastan'gal?" asked Navigator Beaumont.

"It depends on who shot us down," said Sventur coolly. "And that is something we all need to be aware of—we can trust only the officers on this mission. It could be that Fleet Commodore Grizmai will get our reports and act on our behalf, but I don't think we can count on it, you know?"

"That's assuming Grizmai isn't setting us up for the Grands," said Parkerman morosely.

"If he is, he's going about it very strangely," said Sventur. "Remember, your Bunters are to be on guard. We have to make sure that the only enemies we face for the time being are the ones outside." She sighed. "I don't know what to tell you about the other ships. I don't know who is supporting Line Commander Fayrborn."

"You're assuming someone is," her Executive Officer said, an edge in his voice. "That isn't good."

"No, it's not," agreed Sventur. "But we can't

change it now, not while we're down here." She coded a signal. "I've set a special emergency circuit, for your use only. Circuit 17-D will carry *Daichirucken* signals for emergency purposes only. Even the Bunters won't have the code. Keep your com-paks with you at all times, and do not use open channels for emergencies, just this one. Otherwise we could be turning ourselves into targets."

"Sounds great," said Duykster. "Is that all?"

"We better prepare to get out the crawlers and take to the hills. I don't think we can keep our skimmers safe much longer," said Sventur. "We can head back to where the *Suidotal* went down. Group Line Chief Hsuin is probably waiting for us. We'll make a stand there, or work out a plan of attack."

"Unless he's been picked up, him and his crew," said Godwendo with a cynical laugh.

"We can't find out hovering out here," said Sventur. "Ready for egress in one ES hour. Full evacuation and the ship programed for camouflage."

"And what about the Grands? What if we run into them?" Parkerman sounded truly upset at the prospect. "Do we surrender or what?"

"We avoid them," said Sventur, although she hadn't any idea how they were to do it.

The crawlers were equipped with shelters and pre-packaged food as well as enough mid-grade armor to make a short term ground campaign possible. As the five of them rolled out of the bay of the Glavus, the Bunters went about the last stages of preparing the all-terrain vehicles. All the Bunters but the Senior Bunter would travel with their human counterparts in the crawlers: the Senior Bunter would remain with the *Daichirucken*. The Mromrosi announced that he would accompany Group Line Chief Sventur.

"Remember, the *Yamapunkt* will have its crawlers out, too. We're to rendezvous at the *Suidotal*, tomorrow afternoon," said Sventur as she made a last inspection of her Glavus. "If there is any delay, we must inform the *Reiwald*; Acting Line Commander Goriz has to know where we are and when we're ready."

"I don't like the idea that she's staying aloft. It's too risky for us, if she comes under fire." This was the same objection that Parkerman had been making for the last hour and no one paid much attention to him now.

"We're more apt to come under fire," Sventur reminded him as well as the others. "We're the ones on the ground." She checked the two scatter-guns that hung from her belt. "Make sure you're carrying extra ammunition."

"Right you are," said Godwendo, who was in charge of such things. "I've loaded spares into all the crawlers. We should be able to take on a medium-sized ground force."

"Good." Sventur could not get rid of the sense that they were truly on their own, no longer part of anything but their own unit. She looked around at the Glavus and was satisfied that it could not be easily detected from the air, for the shielding screen disguised it from visual and instrumental probing.

They had started the mission with two hundred seventy-seven Petit Harriers to do the job, and now this company stood at forty-three; Sventur did not like the odds, but she had to accept them.

Just before she stepped into the lead crawler, she signaled Emmelien Goriz. "We're about to set off," she said.

"Good," Goriz answered. "We're relying on you. The *Sakibuckt* is going to high orbit, to monitor as much as possible. He'll be using the over-ride emergency channel, if he has to reach any of us. We're going to screen it. Praechee has some tricks up his sleeve that might help us all."

"Wish him luck," said Sventur, thinking of what Pahnahmah Praechee could encounter in orbit— Grands.

"Luck to you, too," said Goriz.

"I'll report in at first light. Don't worry about silence until then." She found it frightening to be out of contact for so long, but she knew it was the only sensible thing to do.

"Carry on, then," said Goriz, and broke their communication.

Sventur left her Glavus for the utilitarian interior of a crawler.

All things considered, the crawlers made good time, heading through the hills, following the signal of the downed *Suidotal*. All night long they trundled along, the growl of their engines loud in the open countryside, which worried Sventur.

"Don't worry. Unless they've set up monitors for sound, it won't make much difference," said Parkerman. "I'm more worried about the Grands in orbit tracking our engine heat. They can do that easily enough." He folded his arms as he stared at the console with its limited display. "I miss the surveills," he said.

"You'll have them again soon enough," said Sventur, looking at the contour lines that appeared, indicating that the ground dropped off steeply not far ahead. "Can we handle that?"

"Oh, yeah," said Parkerman. "We'll rock a little coming down, but it won't be any danger."

"Good," she said, and permitted her Bunter to persuade her to get a few hours' sleep. "Signal me if anything goes wrong, Parkerman," she said as she prepared to go to her bunk. "I'll be back in four hours."

"I'll trade places with you then," said Parkerman, and continued to study the displays. "The link to the other four crawlers is on the left-hand recorder, by the way," he added as she started back in the crawler.

"I'll keep that in mind," she said, feeling very tired.

Parkerman wished her a good sleep, never taking his eyes off the monitors.

Two hours before local sunrise, Sventur was wakened out of her very sound sleep with word that the Executive Officer of the *Sakibuckt* had been found murdered not ten minutes ago.

"Simmon Marillo was discovered with a Drought Central ceremonial dagger in his back, cutting up through the kidney, nicking the aorta and puncturing his right lung," said the Communications Leader, Falmi Brere.

"Where did the ceremonial dagger come from?" asked Sventur, trying to drag herself awake.

"It was Marillo's. He came from Drought Central." There was a short pause. "Whoever killed him was in his quarters last night."

"How many suspects do you have?" she asked, feeling cold in spite of the close interior of the crawler.

"About twenty-eight," he answered. "All those not accounted for on duty are considered suspects, that's what Praechee says. We're running checks with the Bunters, to find out if anyone was noticed—"

"What about Marillo's Bunter?" asked Sventur.

"Disabled. Half its circuits are fried, and don't ask me how that happened. We're assuming the killer disabled the Bunter in order to reach Marillo." He cleared his throat. "We're having real trouble with morale."

"I'm not surprised," said Sventur. "It isn't going to cheer everyone up here, either."

"If we knew where to strike first, we'd be okay. You'd better get something going, for the sake of the whole mission." There was a pause. "I think it's the Grands. I don't think we've got a traitor among us: the Grands have done something."

"It's what the Grands would do," Sventur agreed. "Look how they've led Fayrborn around by the nose."

"Yeah. Well. I'll get back to you. I have to signal the *Yamapunkt* yet."

"Right you are," said Sventur, aware that she would not be able to get back to sleep. She sat up in her bunk, stretching against the stiffness of the morning.

Zameda Lauy-Rei, in the bunk beside Sventur's, opened one eye and regarded her critically. "Not another one."

"On the *Sakibuckt* this time," said Sventur. "Killed with a knife. The Executive Officer, in fact."

Lauy-Rei propped herself on her arm. "Marillo? He's nobody's fool. It's got to be the Grands. Who else could get away with something like this?" She scowled. "Well?"

"It could be, but how are they doing it?" Sventur got out of the bunk and grabbed her wrap. "Fayrborn said he had an ally."

"And you think that's who's doing it?" asked Lauy-Rei.

"I think maybe Fayrborn's figured out a way to make us think so," said Sventur, and headed off for a shower.

By the time she finished, news of Marillo's murder had spread through all the crawlers, and comments were coming back from the others that revealed how much distress the Harriers were feeling.

"I say we get out of here, go find a *Semper* and get one of them back here. I say we stop pogging around and bring in the heavies." Estienne Beaumont was emphatic. He shouted when he spoke and he was not in the mood for an argument. In the crawler immediately behind Sventur's, he took advantage of his position.

"We can turn back. I could order this crawler to turn around, and you wouldn't fire on us to stop us, would you?"

"We've got a job to do first," said Sventur, refusing to get dragged into his posturing. "The *Suidotal* is waiting for us. Group Line Chief Hsuin is waiting for us to get him and his crew out."

"And we rescue them while something's picking off the rest of us?" Beaumont demanded. "What's the sense in that?"

Sventur had no answer for him, but she pointed out that they were on orders from The Hub. "Like it or not, we accepted the assignment, and we'd better do everything we can."

The Mromrosi, who had been listening attentively, now hopped from one of his eight feet to the next, to the next, and the next. "There is a reason you have been sent here," he said, his curls a glistening silver. "This is not merely a question of invaders, or the actions of the Grands. There is another issue."

"It looks that way," said Sventur, who was beginning to wonder if they were being manipulated by Commodore Grizmai. It made sense, she had to admit.

"What are you up to?" growled Executive Officer Duykster as he fumbled his way out of his bunk, his image on the monitor making him look like an undersized brown bear. "What's this about murder?"

"Another one," said Sventur, and filled in as much as she knew. "We need to find out who's doing it."

"Pogging right," said Duykster. "How many Petits will be picked off before we find out who's responsible?"

"I don't know," said Sventur tightly. "As few as possible." She looked over at the Servo-tech working at the Bunter control. "Stepherin, I want you to check all the Bunters, make sure they're running properly, and put them on full alert. They have to stand guard."

"But Marillo's Bunter was fried," said Stepherin reasonably. "I can't keep that from happening to these machines."

"Maybe you can't," Sventur said, "but we can make it a lot harder for someone to break through." She acknowleged the Servo-tech's half-hearted salute. "We're going to have to pick up speed. We've got to reach the *Suidotal* by sundown."

"Your orders indicated that tomorrow morning was—" protested Parkerman only to be cut short.

"Tonight. In case there's another attempt at murder. We don't know if the *Suidotal* is safe." She looked around the cramped driving compartment. "The sooner we're out of here, the better."

Parkerman sighed. "All right. We'll increase speed, if that's what we have to do."

"It's a start," said Sventur.

As they lurched over the hill at sunset they could see the brilliant spatter of disruptor fire, all aimed in the direction of the hidden *Suidotal*.

"Now what?" asked Parkerman as he studied the monitors.

The crawlers idled, their computers digesting the scene below; the Bunters linked with the computers and began to prepare their analyses.

"They're waiting for us," said Sventur, and made sure her messages were coded and screened. "Has anyone located the crawlers from the *Yamapunkt*?" she asked the other four crawlers.

"I think they're two ridges to the west of us," said Navigator Beaumont. "We're getting signals from there."

"Coded?" asked Group Line Chief Sventur quickly.

"And screened. It's got to be them." Beaumont's face on the monitor looked haggard for the forced pace had taken its toll on all of them.

Sventur watched the firing below. "We'd better stay right where we are. Stop, and screen the crawlers," she declared. "Then I want a ground force ready to go as soon as it's dark. I want night gear for everyone and full screen suits. Is that clear? Two Petits from each crawler—that's ten. If anything happens, the rest of you can still get away."

"You're not thinking about going down to the *Suidotal*?" asked Duykster in complete disbelief.

"It's the only thing that makes sense. We'll try to get the crew out." She signaled the Senior Bunter. "We'll need high-energy rations and a stimulant so that we won't fall asleep. The deflector suits will need screening, too, so that they can't track us."

The Mromrosi, who had been listening to all

this with rapt attention, now bounced twice. "You suspect that the attackers are expecting a rescue attempt."

"Yes," said Sventur. "Or they would have blown the *Suidotal* to bits long before now. Those disruptor beams could smash a Glavus with one direct hit." She looked around, considering who should come with her on the mission. "Lauy-Rei, get your equipment ready."

The Protocol Officer grinned in anticipation. "My pleasure, Group Line Chief, and thank you for the opportunity."

Some of the gloom that had hung over the Petits was lifted by Lauy-Rei's enthusiasm.

"I'd like to go along," said the Servo-tech.

"Sorry," Sventur told him. "I need you here. The Bunters are going to have to keep watch of this whole operation, and that means they need to be in perfect working order."

"I'd rather be out there," said Stepherin.

"Not this time," Sventur said. "But do your job well and I'll recommend you for higher rank. That's one way to get into the field properly."

"Right," said Stepherin, and turned back to the Bunters.

"I want one of the monitors on the *Reiwald* at all times," Sventur went on. "As long as we're active down here, the *Reiwald* will be a target. You keep watch on her, and maintain coded contact with Group Line Chief Goriz. If there is any trouble, anything at all, notify me at once."

"But you're going to be out there," said Parkerman.

"It's risky but do it anyway," she said, doing her best to sound calmer than she was. "Look, ever since this mission started we've been reacting—it's time we acted, instead. I need to know what's happening here, and Goriz has to have current information to protect us. Goriz won't be able to help us if we don't report. So it's a greater risk to go on without the contact than to have it. Got it?"

He did not like it and made one last attempt to change her mind. "It might make more sense to send regular crew. Officers like you shouldn't have to—"

"The codes on the other ships recognize the Group Line Chief and Group Chiefs of all the ships. The rest could be fired on because of lack of ship's recognition," she said. "Relax, Stepherin. You'll have your chance."

"I'd like to volunteer to go with you," he said, but more to let her know he was serious than because he expected her to include him in the rescue attempt. "I mean it."

"Maybe later," she said, and went off to get into her class-three combat gear, with screens.

The rescue party assembled in the center of the crawlers. There were ten of them, two from each crawler, and they were all dressed in screened battle garb and armed for skirmishing. There was a small red horsehead on the right epaulet, and gold-and-black flashes on the left. Their weapons were ready, they had rations for two days, and they were determined.

"Pair off," said Sventur as she brought the

group to order. "Lauy-Rei with me; Tsabuki with Ancelott; Mondragon with Hoad; Porree with Crozzer; Godwendo with Thorgemann. Keep your partner with you at all times. No one is to undertake anything alone, is that understood? If something happens to your partner, notify me immediately and *do nothing*. Work with a partner or keep out of the way. I don't want anyone acting solo, not in this situation. Is that clear?"

This was met with mutters of acknowledgement.

"All right. In form. Godwendo and Thorgemann at the rear. The rest of you sort yourselves out for the middle. Double file." She clapped her helmet over her head, checked the communicator, and signaled the rescue party. "Hiking stride."

With her gesture the ten Petit Harriers set out toward the place where the *Suidotal* had been shot down.

"Does anyone know if there are predators around? And are they nocturnal?" asked Godwendo when they had been walking for the greater part of an hour.

"There are some predators," said Sventur, recalling the warnings she had received through her childhood. "The nastiest is something like a wild boar crossed with a leopard, but it isn't found in this part of the country." She, like most members of the Magnicate Alliance, had never seen the animals she mentioned but had done reports on them in school, as she had done reports on dinosaurs.

"Anything else we ought to know about?" Godwendo persisted.

Sventur sighed. "There are several good-sized reptilelike creatures, but they're skittish and they don't get near people if they can help it. There are some nocturnal flyers, not birds and not reptiles but a bit like large bats, that can be dangerous in flocks. They don't come out until after midnight. That's about it. The flyers are called volants; they're about as big as a good-sized owl. They eat meat." In her mind an owl was half her height. "And there's a kind of millipede that has a painful sting that can make you sick, but they don't live in the hills." She had turned and was walking backward. She would have stumbled if Lauy-Rei had not caught her arm and steadied her. "We should reach the *Suidotal* before dark."

"A night rescue could be tricky," warned Moran Thorgemann.

"Don't kid yourself: so could a day one," said Sventur, once again facing forward. She kept to the wooded and brushy parts of the hills, making sure that their movements were as hidden as possible.

By the middle of the afternoon they were a single ridge away from the downed Glavus, and Sventur became more careful, warning her rescue party to proceed with care, making note of all traffic glimpsed in the distance. "They've left the ship intact for one reason."

"That's assuming they've cared enough to look for it," said Godwendo.

"What use is a downed Glavus to them?" asked Thorgemann.

"It's bait for a trap," said Tech Leader Kurdy

Ancelott, sounding disgusted. "And here we are, predictable as rats." He had learned about rats the same way Sventur had learned about wild boars and leopards, and dinosaurs.

"We can't leave them behind," said Sventur reasonably, signaling to the other nine to gather around her. "I need your concentration. We have to be very careful how we approach. They're expecting us to try a rescue. What I hope is that they aren't expecting us to come overland on foot." She tapped her weapons belt. "If we can get in and out without firing, I'll be just as pleased."

"Why?" demanded Crozzer.

"Because they're better armed than we are and it wouldn't take much to wipe us out," she said. "They have disruptors, and I don't have to tell you what they could do to us. Fire draws attention to us, tells them where we are, and they can guess what we're up to."

"Splat," said Medi-Tech Tikin Tsabuki, her comprehensive gesture showing how devastating a single disruptor blast would be. "No chance to get away."

"Precisely. And for that reason, if fire starts, don't stay to fight. Get out of the area if you can, and head back for the ship." Sventur looked from one of the rescue team to the others. "I'll need two of you to stay in the brush to keep watch and provide cover. You stand the greatest risk of getting hit if we have to fight."

Group Chief Godwendo waved. "I'll take it."

"And me," said Tech Leader Ancelott. "We're both armor. We're best trained."

Little as she liked it, Sventur knew that the two were right. "You've got it," she told them. "Make sure you keep covered, suit screens on high and don't use your communicators unless it's absolutely necessary."

"Such as we're under attack," said Godwendo laconically.

"That's it," Sventur assured them both. "Channel 17-D."

"What about the *Yamapunkt*? Aren't we supposed to meet them here?" asked Group Leader Demtro Hoad, introducing a note of concern into their planning.

"Yes," said Sventur.

"Do you still expect them?"

"I hope so. We haven't been signaled that anything's happened to them. They'll probably show up in time." Sventur straightened up. "But that's for later. Right now we have to prepare to get the survivors out of the *Suidotal*."

This time the response was more emphatic and confident.

"Right you are," said Sventur, and gave assignments to all seven Harriers. When she was finished she looked through the brush toward the place where the downed Glavus waited. From her vantage point the ship looked obvious, hardly concealed at all, but she consoled herself with the knowledge that the Glavus was familiar to her and was strange to the Bastan'gal, and possibly less noticeable for that reason. "We'll have to wait a while, until we're into twilight."

"I still don't like doing this at night," said

Ancelott, and added quickly, "Oh, I think you're right, it's the only way we can rescue them, but I don't like it." He scowled at Sventur and glanced up at the sky through the brush.

"The night goggles will—" Sventur began, only to be cut off by Godwendo.

"They'll be fine. But I know how it feels."

"We all do," said Sventur bluntly. "All right. Everyone, nap time. Use your short-term soporifics. You have forty-five ES minutes. Make the most of them."

Grudgingly the others accepted her orders, finding places in the greenery to conceal themselves for a short sleep. Four small, conical monitors were set up to protect them while they recruited their strength for the night and the rescue.

"What do we do if we can't get the crew out?" asked Mondragon.

"It'll depend," said Sventur, being deliberately evasive; she knew that if they could not be saved, the crew of the *Suidotal* would not want to be left alive. Just the thought of what they would have to do made her queasy.

Word came from the *Reiwald* just as the rescue mission was waking that the movement of troops had been spotted not far from the downed *Suidotal*.

"Bastan'gal, by the look of them, moving pretty quickly," reported Communications Leader Vonigal.

"Any Grands with them?" Sventur inquired.

"Not that we can identify, but they could be screened," was the cautious answer.

"Headed this way on purpose," asked Sventur, "or just coming in this direction?"

"It looks like they know what they're doing," said Vonigal. "I'm sorry to tell you."

"Don't be," said Sventur with feeling. "We would have walked into them without the warning. Any idea how they knew to come here?"

"Not any I want to think about," said Vonigal, the emotion he felt reflected in the deepness of his voice; like most Petits from Westward Ho he prided himself on his stoicism, and did not realize how much the pitch of his voice changed when he was distressed.

"Try to find out what happened, anyway," suggested Sventur, though on her own ship it would have been an order.

"We will. One other thing: the Grands have sent down two landing craft that we are aware of. Group Line Chief Goriz thinks it could be a deliberate distraction. They appear to have set down on the smaller southern continent, not where you are." Vonigal reported this factually, but it was clear everyone on the *Reiwald* had been speculating about what the Grands were up to. "So far they've maintained silence, at least as far as our monitors can determine. They could be sending coded zaps or doing screened communications."

"Meaning you think they've been communicating?" asked Sventur.

"That's what I mean. I think all their messages are coded and screened. I think they intend to keep us in the dark as long as they can." Vonigal sounded distressed again, his voice four notes higher than its regular pitch.

"And what about the Bunters?" Sventur inquired. "Can't they pick up anything?"

"Not so far, not . . . anything they're talking about." The last admission was reluctant, and said uneasily, as if the Communications Leader had grown suspicious of the Bunters as well as of the Grands because the machines were not performing as he expected them to. He went on, "The Bunters seem out of their depth on this one. They aren't wired to handle Harriers against Harriers."

"And the Bastan'gal? Are any of them on Truschi Minore or is it just Grands?" asked Sventur, using the Lontaniani's word for the southern continent.

"No Bastan'gal that we've identified," said Vonigal. "The Grands seem to be all by themselves."

"I don't like it," said Sventur.

"Pogging right," said Vonigal. "By the way, something you should know—the *Sakibuckt* reported one of their Bio-Techs found dead about an hour ago. Stabbed with one of the dissecting knives."

"In addition to Marillo?" Sventur was shocked.

"Yes; according to the report the Bio-Tech hasn't been dead more than an hour."

"What the frapping—" she began.

"Group Line Chief Praechee is very worried." This was hardly surprising, but he mentioned it to calm himself.

"He's got a lot of company," she said before she ended their communication.

When she had relayed all the information to the other nine of the rescue party, Sventur

141

remarked, "No matter how bad it looks, we think it's worse than it is because we haven't found out what's going on. And it's worse because we have to wait, and that means we'll dwell on it. So talk it out. Otherwise you won't do your work properly."

"That's the truth," said Thorgemann. "Another murder on the *Sakibuckt*. Pog it!"

"What bothers me," said Tsabuki when the others seemed reluctant to speak, "is that it looks more than ever as if we've got someone in the ranks who—" She broke off. For the first time she missed the Mromrosi. Having the curly little alien along would have made her feel less exposed. As it was, she feared she was at the mercy of her own service.

Her silence was shared by the others; Crozzer looked shamed and Hoad looked angry. Mondragon coughed as if he had a wad of food caught in his throat.

"That's something to remember, that we might be set up," said Sventur. "Like it or not, the Grands are getting Petit help from someone. And someone is killing Petits."

There was a mutter of assent.

"And that means they could have been told everything we're doing." Sventur looked out into the faded afternoon. "If they know we're here, they could—" She stopped herself admitting that they were easy targets.

"We're going to have to do the job quickly and do it right," said Samede Porree. "And not get caught by anyone; not Bastan'gal and not Grands. And maybe not the Mromrosii."

"That's about it," agreed Sventur. She reached down and grabbed her spatter pistol. "Try to keep with these. If we have to use heavier weapons, we're probably lost anyway."

Ancelott chuckled. "Seems peculiar to be hiding from our own forces."

"They aren't our own forces, they're Grands," protested Crozzer.

"They're Harriers," said Lauy-Rei. "That ought to be more important than being Grands or Petits."

"But it isn't," said Tsabuki.

Sventur nodded. "For some reason, the Grands don't want us here on Lontano. But Fleet Commodore Grizmai does. So we better do our work right. We have to answer to the Fleet Commodore, not to our Big Brothers," she reminded them, using the pejorative nickname the Petits had given the Grands, as the Grands sometimes referred to the Petits as Step-Children.

"Whatever that means," said Ancelott merrily.

"We'll start with the *Suidotal*," said Hoad. "And if we live through that, maybe we can find out what's going on here."

This time the rescue party was more encouraged, most of them slapping their right hand on their left shoulder in salute.

Sventur peered out through the brush. "I don't know if anyone's left alive, but that's what matters, living Petits. If we're too late, then get any information you can and get out of there. Godwendo, Ancelott, you keep the rear guard, and make sure you put your helmets on full scan. I don't want mechanicals sneaking up on us while we're looking for biologicals. In fact, I don't want anything sneaking up on us."

"So right," said Godwendo, taking a wide-beam paralyzer from her hip-pak. "This will stop most of them."

"Does that thing work on Bastan'gal physiology?" Thorgemann asked.

"We'll find out," Godwendo assured him.

Now all of the rescue party laughed softly but with the keyed-up intensity of those preparing for a serious fight. Only Mondragon sounded truly nervous; the others were accustomed to the excitement and contained it better than the young man from Chalot on his first mission.

"All right then," said Sventur as she allowed herself to be optimistic for the first time since they arrived at Lontano. "Go to the parts of the ship where you are normally assigned. You'll know how to check over everything. Do it quickly, then come to the bridge unless we're under attack. If we are, go to the emergency vane exit, and leave that way."

"What about the crew? Do we gather them over here with us?" demanded Ancelott.

"If it looks like the best way to handle this," said Sventur, adjusting her weapons belt. "I want all of you to keep low, stay close to the brush. Approach the ship from the north, and go in the rear entrance. That's the one that's least likely to be damaged." She lowered her helmet and put the lenses on full power. The fading shadows of night vanished and the *Suidotal* lay as if bathed in bright floodlights.

Beside her, Lauy-Rei pulled her stunner and moved the setting on full.

Very slowly, Sventur led the way to the edge of the brush, taking care to stay in the shadows as much as possible. She ducked and bobbed as she moved, hoping this would make identifying them more difficult for anyone watching. As they reached the edge of the wreck, she motioned all the Petits to crouch. "One at a time," she whispered, knowing that their helmets would pick up her voice. "Partners two strides apart, ten strides between pairs. Everyone, be ready."

There was a brief silence as the rest made a last check, then she heard the two tongue-clicks that served to signal ascent.

"Lauy-Rei, here we go," she said, and broke from cover, keeping her head down. Out of the corner of her eye she saw Lauy-Rei come after her.

They reached the aft vane of the *Suidotal*, and pressed the emergency code into the exposed plate.

Lauy-Rei came up beside her, weapons at the ready.

Nothing happened.

Sventur pressed the code a second time. There was a metallic groan, but the hatch remained firmly closed.

"Pog it!" Sventur whispered, and coded the over-ride emergency series, which triggered the explosive bolts on the hatch. She ducked back, and pulled Lauy-Rei down beside her.

Seven seconds later the hatch flew off, clanging away into the brush.

"So much for our unannounced arrival," said Lauy-Rei in an undervoice.

Mondragon and Thorgemann had reached them now, and were hunkered down at guard.

"Ready to go in?" asked Sventur, and before she could think about the danger too much, she reached up, grabbed the edge of the hatch, and vaulted inside the ship, coming to rest in a huddled ball at the side of the main corridor.

Lauy-Rei was right behind her.

The whump and sizzle of disruptor fire came almost at once. There were two muffled screams in the brush.

"Pogging sperks!" whispered Lauy-Rei.

The two of them crouched in the bent corridor, waiting for a response from the ship.

Cautiously Sventur rose, her helmet magnifying the low light in the corridor to moderate brightness. She found the nearest comm-patch on the wall, and tried to code in.

"I don't think it's working," whispered Lauy-Rei beside her.

"No, neither do I. It looks as if the whole ship is on subsistence power only. What a pogging mess." Sventur glanced around as Mondragon dropped into the corridor.

"Thorgemann was hit. Outside. He can't make it inside." Mondragon was pale and shaken, but he did not cave in. "That blast. The disruptor beam caught his arm."

Sventur heard this out in silence, then cursed. "His suit still working?"

"He's sealed off, if that's what you mean. The shock isn't too bad, not so long as the suit is doing its job. Hoad's checking him out." Mondragon scowled. "What about the rest?"

"We'll have to see," said Sventur, and started forward.

She passed two motionless Bunters on the way, and had a moment of distress as she realized they could not be made operable, not with the ship on subsistence power only.

There were two emergency hatches secured across the corridor, and each one had to be blown open by coding the explosive bolts.

By now there were six of Sventur's party inside the *Suidotal*. There were two casualties—Thorgemann and Tsabuki—outside the ship, and two—Godwendo and Ancelott—were guarding the rear along with the injured Petits. Which left Sventur, Lauy-Rei, Crozzer, Hoad, Mondragon, and Porree to bring out the entire remaining crew of the *Suidotal*.

Suddenly the ship lurched as a disruptor beam struck the top vane, rocking the Glavus violently.

The rescue party scrambled for footing, hands lifted to protect their heads from impact as two of the ceiling panels fell with a nerve-rattling crash that echoed through the ship like the tolling of tuneless bells.

"Is everyone all right?" Sventur asked when the ship was still again.

All five reported themselves all right.

"Let's keep going, then," said Sventur, hating the sense of doom that hung over her.

"Can't you signal the bridge, to let them know we're coming?" inquired Porree.

"Not with the ship on subsistence power, no," answered Sventur, and got ready to blow the last set of bolts. "As soon as we're through, go to your areas and check the ship out. Make sure you record everything."

With that, she programmed the third hatch's explosive bolts.

As the hatch ripped into flying sections of metal, four Petit Harriers appeared in the passage beyond, weapons at the ready.

Sventur stepped forward very carefully, her hands partly raised. "Magnicate Alliance Petit Harrier Group Line Chief Leatris Sventur of the *Daichirucken*, here to collect you."

The nearest officer lowered his weapon at once. "Executive Officer Khirmian TeRoumei, Group Line Chief. And very glad to see you." He signaled the other three to put their stunners aside.

"Same here, Executive Officer," said Sventur, motioning to the others. "How bad is it?"

"Not good," said TeRoumei. "We haven't been able to get the ship's systems working at all. We've only had subsistence power since the crash. Which means no Bunters and no ship's services."

"Casualties?" asked Sventur as her rescue party came up beside her.

"More than we'd like," said TeRoumei. "We had three fatalities when we went down, another four since, and there are a dozen injured from broken bones to concussions to cuts and bruises." He pointed toward the bridge. "Group Line Chief Hsuin is waiting for you. He has a broken leg."

"Great," said Sventur, thinking of the difficulty they would have getting him out of the ship and back to safety. "Any other casualties?"

"What do you mean?" asked TeRoumei. "What kind of casualties are you talking about?"

"No . . . murders?" she asked diffidently, doing what she could to make the question less troublesome.

"Murders? Plural?" repeated TeRoumei. "You mean there have been more?"

"Unfortunately, yes," said Sventur, and motioned her squad to follow her. "Let's get this rescue going."

The entire ship rocked again as another disruptor bolt shuddered the frame of the Glavus. The rescue party crouched but TeRoumei hardly bothered.

"Have you had to put up with much of this?" Sventur asked when the *Suidotal* was still again. "You don't look as if the ship has taken many hits."

"We haven't been attacked. Not until this afternoon," said TeRoumei, and with a shove opened the hatch to the bridge.

Group Line Chief Hsuin Xanitan sat with his splinted leg propped on one of the stools. Beside him the Mromrosi waited, a soft mauve color, his single green eye bent on the new arrivals.

The rest of the bridge crew looked exhausted but in reasonable shape. Only Tech-Leader Wharton's station was empty, and by the way the rest avoided looking at it, Sventur assumed that Wharton had been one of the casualties.

"We're glad to see you, Sventur," said Hsuin. "What took you so long?"

"We couldn't find a place to park," Sventur replied in the same exaggerated coolness of manner that Hsuin used.

"Then it's going to be a hike?" he asked, looking apprehensive behind his bravado. He indicated his leg. "I might need to be picked up later."

"Sorry, but it looks as if you're going to have to run for it with the rest of us," she declared, then indicated her team. "We'll get you out of here when it's good and dark."

Hsuin shook his head. "I don't think so. We've been under lights since we went down, on full all the time. The Bastan'gal are dug in around us."

"So we assumed," said Lauy-Rei. "But keeping you in the light—isn't that a little extreme?"

"It is most untypical," said the Mromrosi suddenly, rocking back on six of its eight little heels.

"You mean they don't usually put a downed ship in bright lights?" asked Sventur, a cold feeling spreading through her. "You're saying that only the Grands do that?"

"It is a pattern with them," said the Mromrosi.

"Yeah," said Sventur, and noticed how many of the Petits exchanged angry and uneasy looks.

"So we're in a difficult situation," said Hsuin in his best laconic manner. "And I don't know how we're going to get out, not with the Grands after us."

"You don't know they're after us, not for sure," said Communications Leader Alik Ammir. His face was pale and his eyes had deep rings around them, suggesting long, sleepless hours.

"Yes, we do," said Sventur directly. "There's no doubt."

Hsuin made a fatalistic gesture. "So where does that put us? Other than in the line of fire?"

"That's it," said Sventur, and saw how disheartened the rest looked. "But there's one thing in our favor—they aren't expecting us to do anything. They think we're not up to taking them on."

"How can we?" asked Hsuin, looking around his bridge. "If we get out of here, they'll pick us off. And they can blast us to fractured atoms while we're here, any time they want."

"Exactly. So we might as well try to turn the tables," said Sventur. "What have we got to lose?"

"You have a point," Hsuin conceded.

They had improvised a sling between Group Chief Miya Maht and Navigator Betness Gos-Raidan that allowed them to carry Group Line Chief Hsuin standing up, hands free to aim.

"I wish we had a couple Bunters working," said Hsuin as the two women steadied him between them.

"Worry about that later, when we get back to the *Daichirucken*," advised Sventur.

"I still think we should have let the *Yamapunkt* know what we're doing. If they get here and find us gone . . ." Hsuin rubbed his face with his free hand. "They're going to have to face the Grands and the Bastan'gal on their own."

"If they get here," said Sventur, motioning toward the emergency hatch in the vane. "And one look ought to discourage them." There were two steep ladders that had been lowered and now they were starting out of the stricken Glavus.

"You think they'll be attacked?" asked Ammir, following Porree up the nearer ladder.

"It's a possibility," said Sventur.

"But you think it could be something else, don't you?" asked Lauy-Rei in her steady way. "You're convinced there's a Grands agent with us."

"Somewhere in the mission, yes," she answered grimly. "And so do you."

"True," Lauy-Rei admitted as she started to make a place for the *Suidotal* crew to gather to leave. "We're going to have to move fast once we're out."

Above them TeRoumei and Hoad worked on the hatch to release it, both cursing as they struggled.

"It is a surprising effort you have made, Group Line Chief Sventur," said the Mromrosi, coming back from traipsing along beside the wounded and injured as they approached the bridge. He was a brilliant shade of raspberry. "It is unexpected. It is daring."

"It's part of the job," said Sventur, her face revealing little emotion. She did not entirely trust the curly alien now that they were as cut off as they were. "You better get up the ladder, in case you need help."

"Oh, it is no difficulty for me," said the Mromrosi, sounding amused. He hopped forward, grabbed the lowest rung by one of his eight feet, and swung himself vigorously upward, seizing the next rung. He looked like an enormous pom-pom swaying up a huge pair of shoelaces.

Sventur stared at the Mromrosi, for she had never seen one climb a ladder before. She heard the others chuckle, and nodded her approval;

anything that improved morale was important now. She signaled the assembled crew members of the *Suidotal.* "You know what you have to do."

"What about the two who are too badly wounded?" asked one of the Bio-Techs as more than a dozen of the *Suidotal's* crew started toward the ladders, ready to climb.

It was a question she did not want to answer. "You know what regulations say."

"But they're part of our crew," the Bio-Tech protested.

"They're not supposed to be taken captive," said Sventur, wondering how she would feel if she were one of those who would have to be left behind, painless, lethal capsules ready to be put to final use.

"But they don't have to—" the Bio-Tech said. "Wouldn't the Grands take them? What's wrong leaving them to the Grands?"

"It's orders, and we're under disruptor fire," said Sventur more firmly. "We don't have a lot of choice."

The Bio-Tech accepted this scornfully. "Sure, Group Line Chief. Makes lots of sense to me."

"It's orders," Sventur repeated.

"Right," said the Bio-Tech, and started up the ladder. "I'd carry them on my back if I could."

"And you'd die with them," said Sventur, knowing it was the truth.

As if to underscore her words, another disruptor bolt slammed into the side of the Glavus, rocking it dangerously, sending those waiting to leave tottering into one another.

"You're wasting time," Sventur warned the

Bio-Tech, and motioned to more of the *Suidotal*'s crew to move.

"They're just teasing us," said Lauy-Rei softly as she came up to Sventur. "They could turn this whole ship to slag in one shot if they wanted to."

"I know," said Sventur with a nervous frown.

"They could be waiting to round us up outside," Lauy-Rei pointed out.

"I realize that. But what else can I do? We have to get out of here if we can." Sventur put her hand on her stunner and looked around the steadily emptying bridge. "If we don't—" She stopped, then made herself continue. "If we don't do what Fleet Commodore ordered, we're going to be in more trouble than ever. So we've got to try."

"If that's what you want," said Lauy-Rei, willing to obey in spite of her doubts.

"It's the only course open," said Sventur, watching as the escape continued.

"Do you wonder," said Lauy-Rei softly, "why they didn't try to get out on their own?"

"Not with those disruptors out there, no. I probably would have done the same thing—kept my head down and waited," said Sventur, although now that it was mentioned, she did wonder. "Better order a check of the ship's computers from the *Reiwald*—after we get away."

Lauy-Rei nodded and started toward the ladders. More than half the crew of the *Suidotal* was out of the ship now, and those who could leave were ready to go.

"I don't like the way this place feels," Sventur

admitted to Lauy-Rei, glancing around uneasily. "And I don't mean the disruptors. I mean—"

"No; I know what you mean," said Lauy-Rei. She indicated the line of immobile Bunters at the rear of the bridge. "They're spooky."

"That they are," Sventur agreed, and very nearly shuddered as she watched them, unable to shake the sense that the cyborgs were about to move.

When the next disruptor bolt detonated, a portion of the forward surveills shattered, splintering all over the bridge as the bow of the Glavus buckled.

The Petit Harriers on the ladders clung to them desperately as the ship juddered.

"Their aim is improving," said Lauy-Rei, concealing her fright with sarcasm.

"They know we're getting out," Sventur said, and motioned to the rest to keep moving. "And I'm worried."

"You're afraid they'll pick us off?" asked Lauy-Rei.

"Or round us up, or who knows what." Sventur thought again of the wounded about to be abandoned, and she concealed her trembling.

"That's part of the risk," said Lauy-Rei. "But what else can we do?" With that, she started toward the ladders where the rest of the rescuers waited. "Group Line Chief?"

"In a couple seconds, when the rest of you are out," she said, and made a last circuit of the damaged bridge. She noticed that the greatest destruction was to the computer units, leaving little behind but fused silicates.

Another disruptor blast wrecked what little remained of the undercarriage of the Glavus, and as a result the ship canted farther onto its side, throwing the few Petits remaining on the bridge into confusion and disorder.

"Hang on!" Sventur shouted. "Everyone! Hang on!"

The order was needless, for that was precisely what all crew members were doing. Two hung from their arms at the top of the ladders, clinging to them as they swung their legs attempting to find purchase.

"You better get out of here," said Sventur to Lauy-Rei. "I want you to get everyone under cover as fast as possible. I've got one last thing I have to do."

"The remaining wounded?" said Lauy-Rei.

Sventur winced. "It's their option." She straightened up, thinking of what she would do if she were in the place of the stricken Petits. "There's a good chance the Bastan'gal will attack when they think they can."

Once again the remaining members of the rescue team were gingerly picking their way up the ladders, headed for the damaged hatch, weapons within reach.

"If they haven't done it already and are just stringing us along," added Lauy-Rei.

"Spoken like a true Protocol Officer," said Sventur.

"Yeah. Well." Lauy-Rei went to the nearest ladder. "It'll hold a little longer if they don't fire again."

"It ought to," said Sventur. "Get everyone under cover," she repeated.

"How long do I wait, if I have to wait?" asked Lauy-Rei as she resigned herself to Group Line Chief Sventur's orders.

"Give me five minutes. If you don't see me or receive my signal, start back. Keep watch for the *Yamapunkt*. We were supposed to have help from her before now."

"That's Fayrborn's ship," said Lauy-Rei as she started up the ladder.

"It's Boro Omerrik's ship now," corrected Sventur. "And he's good at his job."

"Unlike Fayrborn," said Lauy-Rei, making good progress up the canted ladder.

Sventur turned away and headed back down the corridor toward the little sick bay where the most dangerously wounded lay. She carefully made herself think of other things than her mission with the wounded.

They were still, most of them no more than partly conscious. They were monitored by small machines. Sventur could see the capsules in their hands. She paused in the open door, watching them.

"The ship is nearly empty and the enemy is coming," she said with difficulty, her throat suddenly too dry. "We can't get you out, not in the condition you are in. You are in danger of capture, or taking direct assault. Your capsules are ready, if you decide to use them. If you decide not to, you are warned that we will probably not be able to make a second rescue attempt." She had been taught long since about this warning, but never thought she would have to give it.

The injured were silent but for the sounds made by their monitoring machines.

"Well, it's up to you," she said, and turned away.

She had almost reached the bridge again when something occurred to her, something so outrageous that she decided it just might have a chance to succeed. She stepped into the Transmissions room and quickly encoded two zaps, firing them off in two micro-condensed bursts.

"With any luck," she whispered, "they won't be noticed, not with all the fighting going on down here."

As if to confirm this, another disruptor blast shook the *Suidotal*, this time ripping open most of the starboard side.

Sventur ran for the ladders and pulled herself up them while the ship shuddered and moaned like an animal in its death-throes.

Night had settled in over this part of Lontano. The undergrowth and trees were nothing more than dense shapes some undetermined distance away. The brilliant illumination that held the *Suidotal* like a specimen on a slide was as limited as it was intense, making the darkness more complete.

She was not more than a dozen steps away from the Glavus, at the very edge of the brightness, when a tremendous concussion lifted her from her feet and flung her into the branches of the nearest cover.

Behind her the *Suidotal* glowed fantastically as the disruptor at last hit with full power, tearing the ship to molten splinters.

3

Dazed, Sventur found herself on all fours trying to figure out how she got there. Her head rang and her eyes were not working quite right. She could smell smoke and the greater odor of hot alloys. Mechanically she began to move away from the heat, uncertain of where she was going.

Then Tech Leader Kurdy Ancelott was at her side, shouting at her to be heard. "Come on, Sventur! We've got to get out of here. The crawlers are waiting."

"Right," she said, amazed at how she croaked when she spoke.

Provisions Leader Sather Crozzer joined them, grinning his ferocious Standbyer grin. He took hold of her arm and hauled her upright. "You were the one who said we had to get moving," he reminded her, and set about getting her through the underbrush. His expression was set and his eyes were very bright with purpose. He refused to look over his shoulder.

"Is the fire spreading?" Sventur asked when they had gone far enough to escape the heat at their backs.

"Some. Not enough to worry us yet. We've got the crew just over the ridge, including the Group Line Chief. He's not in great shape, but he's holding on. We're getting the wounded aboard the crawlers, for speed and protection. Okay? Hsuin's been protesting being taken along. He thinks he'll slow us down too much. He's having trouble with his leg and can't walk at all." Crozzer was looking tired himself, and there were smudges on his face from the fire and smoke.

"He'll be in the crawlers; it doesn't matter," said Sventur, her head clearing now. "The crew can take care of him, even without the Bunters."

"It's harder without Bunters," said Crozzer.

"All their Bunters are down," said Sventur by way of explanation.

Ancelott grunted. "He said that. Must have been hard, working without Bunters."

"They have . . . had wounded on board. Without Bunters, they . . . had only monitors." Sventur hated to think of those unfortunate crew members who had been lost with the ship. She hoped that the end—from the disruptor or their capsules—and been swift and merciful.

"A bad situation. Our Bunters will have to work overtime, once we get back to the ship. We'll manage until then," said Ancelott, and tugged more firmly on Sventur's arm. "The Bastan'gal will start patrolling as soon as the fire's out. We'd better be out of here."

"No argument," said Sventur, and shook herself free of the guiding hold of her two men. "Just tell me which way to go."

"Toward the ridge," said Crozzer.

Without another word, Sventur lengthened her stride and pressed her way through the underbrush and the night.

In the last three hours they had covered a considerable distance back toward the *Daichirucken*, the crawlers keeping pace with those on foot, occasionally providing something to ride when the ground became too rough for those on foot who had been displaced from the interiors by the injured. Only the Mromrosii seemed unaffected by the trek; whether in the crawlers or with those walking, they were unrelentingly active and cheerful.

They had almost reached their Glavus when the *Yamapunkt* appeared, circling overhead with most navigational lights off except for the identifying green-and-purple flashes on the rear vane.

"About time," said Crozzer to Sventur as they looked up.

"I wonder where they were?" said Bio-Tech Mondragon.

"Probably lost, or evading Bastan'gal," said Sventur, wanting to end speculation as quickly as possible. "Maybe providing a diversion."

"Or Grands, they might have been leading the Grands astray," said Lauy-Rei from the forward command seat of the front crawler.

The two Mromrosii were huddled in the corner of the crawler, one of them a luminous puce, the other a mauvey-grey. Their high, fast squeaks and clicks were just loud enough to be noticeable and mildly distracting.

"We don't know that the Grands have taken an active part in this. All we know is that Line Commander Fayrborn has run off to their ship. The rest is guesswork." Sventur knew this was useless as she spoke, and had her certainty rewarded by Ancelott.

"We can make some pretty good guesses,

Group Line Chief. Better than good." Ancelott's glower deepened and he added, "Pogging Grands. They did this to us. Somehow, they did it."

"Save it for later, when we're safe," recommended Communications Leader Parker Parkerman with an annoyed gesture in Ancelott's direction. "Right now we need help. And the *Yamapunkt* is a Petit ship."

"I don't want to get anyone into trouble," said Sventur with real concern as the *Yamapunkt* hovered overhead. "We know what we think is going on, but if we start making accusations, the Grands could make us look pretty pogging foolish if they have an answer on record."

"And you know sperking well there is an explanation on record," added Lauy-Rei. "And I would like to know what it is."

"How long before they land?" asked Mondragon. "And where are they going to land?"

"I don't know," said Sventur. "Maybe someone in the crawlers has had contact with them while we were gone?" She looked around, waiting for a response from her crews.

"All silent," said Parkerman.

Mondragon sighed. "I wish they'd reached us before now."

"I don't think so," said Lauy-Rei. "It could provide a signal for the enemy to home on."

"True," said Sventur, and took a chance with her communicator, ordering the crawlers to halt for the moment, thinking quickly. "We need a break in any case," she added, "*Yamapunkt* here or not. And the wounded need help."

"That's the truth," said Lauy-Rei, and for the

first time since their rescue mission began she looked truly tired.

As the crawlers pulled into a circle, the *Yamapunkt* dropped lower, still hovering over them.

"What's happening?" Godwendo inquired from the crawler. "What's going on?"

"We're taking a break," Sventur alerted them all. "If it looks safe, we'll arrange for the *Yamapunkt* to take the wounded."

"Right," approved Crozzer. "Get the Bunters to take care of them, that's the way."

"That's what I thought," said Sventur. "We're in no position to give any treatment—that's Bunters' work, in any case. The sooner the wounded are in their hands, the better."

Crozzer gave a single nod. "Getting on it."

"What word do we have from them?" asked Sventur, looking over at Lauy-Rei. "Anything coming through?"

"Old code," said Lauy-Rei, examining the pattern on the communications display. "Their ship's damaged. They're going to outside voice hailers."

As soon as she said this, a huge, artificial baritone boomed down from overhead. "Good to see you, Petits."

For some reason she could not explain, the phrase bothered Sventur. It was not the blatantly imitation sound of the voice, but something more, something she could not identify. All the relief that had washed over her left her at once. She pressed the emergency-shield trigger before she used her hailer. "We have wounded, *Yamapunkt*."

Both Mromrosii capered toward the communications display, one of them now bright pink, the other chartreuse.

"We'll take them off your hands. You can have a ride back to your ship, as well, if you like. We can handle a double load that far," offered the manufactured voice.

"Good of you to say so," Sventur responded. "But we don't want to abandon the crawlers unless we have to." She looked around the cramped command center, realizing that some of the others were disappointed to hear her give up the advantages of speed and comfort.

The falsely human voice sounded disappointed. "You're probably being too cautious, Group Line Chief Sventur. Let us take you aboard."

"Ommerik?" Sventur inquired, wondering that the Executive Officer of the *Yamapunkt* would use a ship-created voice to speak with her.

"Communications Leader Gara Gaikhu," the voice corrected, and gave Sventur something of a shock, for it seemed strange that the gorgeous and flirtatious Gaikhu would ever disguise her identity, let alone her sex.

"Gaikhu," said Sventur. "Where's Ommerik?" She felt herself grow cold as she asked the question. Executive Officer Ommerik was in charge of the *Yamapunkt* and he should be the one speaking to her, even though Gaikhu was in charge of communications. "I want to make a report to him, so you can relay it to Goriz."

"It's a bad thing about Ommerik," said Gaikhu, still in the communicator-generated male voice of the ship. "We found him two hours ago, dead.

One of the pitons from the surface supplies had been . . . He was stabbed."

"Pogging bonocks!" Sventur swore.

"His Bunter found him," said Gaikhu through the machine.

"You made your report yet?" Sventur asked, aware that many of those in the crawlers were listening attentively.

"How could such a misfortune befall Executive Officer Ommerik?" asked the pink Mromrosi. "Surely there has been a breach of security."

"About to zap The Hub. Coded, of course," said Gaikhu. "For the time being, Diam Bontorn is in charge up here; another Lontaniano, like you."

Sventur knew the Protocol Officer of the *Yamapunkt* slightly, so said, "Not bad."

The voice blared away. "So you know we can manage it. Send the wounded up and we'll get them into care. If you insist on finding your way back, go ahead, but let us take the wounded."

"It'd make more sense for you to send down two Bunters," said Sventur, knowing full well this was an absurd suggestion. She was unable to shake the certainty that there was something very wrong aboard the *Yamapunkt*. Too much had happened on that ship and in too short a time—it rankled. She chided herself inwardly for such unnecessary caution, but continued to hold to her conviction. "Two Bunters will be enough. Most of the injuries are not serious."

One of the Mromrosii was now a nasty shade of milky-peach, his green eye faded from emerald to bottle. According to the Mromrosii, this happened when they did their version of meditation. The other was a neutral khaki color with faint rosy points on the tips of his proliferation of curls.

There was a pause, then the large voice said, "Right you are. Two Bunters."

Sventur was shocked that Gaikhu had not challenged her request, for it was a radical departure from standard procedure, and more astonished when she saw two Bunters being lowered to them on gravity pads.

A few of the Petits gathered outside the crawlers stared at the cyborgs in amazement.

"You mind telling me why you're doing this, Group Line Chief?" Protocol Officer Lauy-Rei whispered to Sventur.

"Later," Sventur said.

The Bunters came to rest in the middle of the crawlers. As soon as the pads were down, the big machines activated themselves. One trundled toward Sventur's crawler and one to Godwendo's. They moved with steady purpose, as Bunters always did.

"We're getting back to Goriz," said Gaikhu, still deep and masculine-sounding on the hailer. "If you're sure there's nothing else we can do?"

"This is great, *Yamapunkt*. Thanks for everything. See you in a few hours," said Sventur, watching the Glavus rise. Then she shifted her attention and immediately deactivated the communications bank. "Everyone out of here. Out of the crawlers. Now. All crawlers empty. We're going on foot. Lauy-Rei, make sure we have a zap board with us, just in case." Energy fizzed through her, more than she could ever remember feeling. "Three ES minutes."

There was a hint of protest but it was cut short by Lauy-Rei who snapped, "You heard her. Three minutes and out."

Group Leader Demtro Hoad knelt down beside Sventur in the brush beyond the circle of the crawlers. "Do you mind telling me why we're doing this?" he asked in his most reasonable tone. Behind him one of the Mromrosii glistened the color of tarnished silver.

"I, too, am curious about it," said the Mromrosi.

Sventur had an answer for them both. "Simple precaution. Think a little. The *Yamapunkt* gave the Grands a huge, flashing beacon to where we are, and the Bastan'gal probably are aware of it, too," she said steadily. "Between all the noise and the long hovering, there probably isn't a Grand from here to the *Mon Droit Cassiopeia* who doesn't know the location of those crawlers."

Hoad shook his head. "Come on, Sventur. You don't really think that—"

He was cut short as a shattering beam of light lanced down from the sky, incinerating the crawlers as it touched them.

"Soko!" exclaimed Hoad.

"Exactly," said Sventur.

The half-dozen irregular moonlets known as Le Node bumbled along through the sky at the end of the night. The small party of Petit Harriers used what little extra light Le Node provided to increase their speed over the rough terrain.

"I don't know how much longer we can keep going," said Group Leader Sather Crozzer. "Even the Bunters aren't holding up well. And Group Line Chief Hsuin can't take much more."

Sventur sighed, for her feet had been aching through the last hour. She let herself come to a halt. "All right. There's a hollow down the hill." She pointed away into the darkness. "We can rest there for a while, but only for a while. If the Grands aren't chasing us, you can be pogging certain the Bastan'gal are."

Lauy-Rei, who had been scouting ahead on the right, came stumbling back toward them. "He's right, Sventur. We can't keep this pace up much longer, dawn or no dawn. We need rest, especially the injured. We have to let the Bunters get to work on them."

"You have a point," said Sventur, accepting the inevitable and needing to sit down long enough to ease her feet.

"We're all exhausted, Group Line Chief," said Mondragon, his voice very weak. His bruised shoulder had swollen and given him a hunchback appearance. "I know I have to rest." He stared at her, then dared to ask his question. "Why wouldn't you let us go aboard the *Yamapunkt*?"

The two Mromrosii frolicked up to them, one robin's-egg blue, the other periwinkle. "Yes, Group Line Chief, we of the Emerging Planet Fairness Court would like to hear your answer."

There were mutters seconding the question as the rest came nearer. "Yeah, Sventur," said Navigator Gos-Raidan. "Hsuin needs rest and care. You didn't let him have it."

"I didn't think he'd get it on the *Yamapunkt*," she said slowly. "The ship was too visible. Anyone could make it a target, and that wouldn't do anyone any good." She shoved her free hand deep into her cargo pocket and pulled out two more sheets of high-nutrition rations. "Here," she offered.

A few of the Petits pulled off sections of the concentrated food—it was tasteless as waste-paper but incredibly nourishing—and obediently chewed.

"At least we have Bunters to carry Hsuin and Thorgemann," said Ancelott, who was nursing a bad abrasion down the right side of his face. "We couldn't have come this far without them."

Parkerman coughed once, and said, "This isn't some kind of test, is it?"

"But why did we have to come this far?" protested Miya Maht. "All right, I admit that the *Yamapunkt* could be an obvious target, but —"

"Remember what happened to the crawlers," advised Porree. "It could have been us if Sventur hadn't ordered us out."

"Granted," said Maht impatiently. "But that doesn't mean we have to wander all over the continent in order to get out of range. One of those orbital ships could pick us off in ten seconds if they decided to stop us."

"And that's why we've kept moving," said Sventur as she tore at the rations sheet with her teeth. "Once they realize we weren't in the crawlers, they'll probably begin searching for us. The farther away we are from where they expect to find us, the better chance we have of surviving," she said in her most reasonable tone. "I'm trying to buy us a little time and get us out of the danger zone if I can."

"What good will that do?" Ancelott asked.

"I don't know yet," Sventur admitted. She would not tell anyone about the coded zaps she had sent from the *Suidotal* just before she left it.

Most of the Petit Harriers nodded, though Executive Officer Khirmian TeRoumei looked seriously displeased and Group Leader Kurdy Ancelott swore in Hathaway jargon which few of the rest understood.

The periwinkle Mromrosi, who had scampered along beside them without complaint, now spoke up. "It is a circumspect decision you have made, Group Line Chief Sventur. A wise leader takes necessary precautions, no matter how distasteful. You have very good sense and better instincts, which are rarer. Therefore I must suppose your actions will continue to be in the best interests of the Petit Harriers under your command, and endorse your plan." He turned a deep golden-russet while he said this; Sventur wondered what the color signified.

"True," said the robin's-egg blue one. "Sventur has shown an excellent appreciation of the ratio of risk. This is most reassuring, you may be confident of it." At the end of this he faded to a cloudy grey,

"Well," she said, a little astonished by such approval, and so clearly explained, "then my instincts and my feet say that we take a three-hour break, soporifics for those who need them. The Bunters can use the time to tend to the injuries." She indicated the hollow again. "We should be able to walk that distance in twenty ES minutes without going too fast for safety. Just remember the slope is slippery."

The others nodded, and this time none of them appeared to object. For once Ancelott said nothing.

"All right," said Sventur, and made herself take the first step.

They were all making their way down the hill, cursing as the treacherous footing skittered and slipped, threatening to send them all toppling. Only the two Bunters made their way without mishap, their stabilizers compensating for the precarious route.

A little over half-way to the hollow, a number of large, winged shapes began to flicker ahead in the darkness. They rose over the Petit Harriers and circled, giving a strange cry like the sound of a nail scraped over stone.

"Volants!" exclaimed Sventur, and she began to run, trying to keep her balance as she went, her arms windmilling as much to keep the flying carnivores away as to aid in her remaining upright.

"They eat meat?" Crozzer shouted.

"Yes!" Sventur answered, and tripped on a loose rock. She strained, floundered, almost dropped her zap board, but stayed on her feet, her ankles so wrenched that she feared she would have to cut her boots off.

"How do you stop them?" shouted TeRoumei.

"You don't. You run," Sventur replied.

"Volants!" caroled the Mromrosii as they capered over the small cascade of dirt and pebbles that marked the path of the Harriers' run.

The Petits were in full rout, rushing as fast as they could. Two of them fell and picked themselves up again, but one—Group Chief Takenyi Borisov of Vladimir—was raked on the face and neck by the volants. Zameda Lauy-Rei succeeded in knocking one of the reptilelike creatures out of the air with a fortunate hand-to-hand combat blow.

The Bunters kept on their way steadily, using one set of arms to flail at the volants as if they were pesky irritations instead of carnivorous predators. They supported their Petit Harrier charges without mishap.

By the time they reached the shelter of the trees, Kurdy Ancelott had also been badly raked on his head and was swearing in profane and unrepeating determination, mixing Harrier and Hathaway idiom in creative abandon.

Under the trees Sventur at last gathered all the Petits together once more, and with the help of the Mromrosii was able to establish a make-shift camp. It was little more than a cleared circle in the midst of the trees, but it was protected enough for the remainder of the night.

"I will observe, and the Bunters will do the rest," the Mromrosii assured Sventur, both of them a coral color. "You may have your needed rest."

It was an effort for Sventur to keep her eyes open, for she had just taken a two-hour soporific.

"Thanks," she said, her tongue feeling thick. "Good of you to do it. You must be as tired as we are."

"Yes, it is, isn't it, good of us. And our fatigue is not as yours," said the Mromrosi standing closer to her, going a beneficent shade of mint green that was wholly lost on Sventur in the darkness. He watched her until he was satisfied she was asleep, then strolled around the perimeter of the camp, his single green eye turned on the Bunters. His fellow-Mromrosi remained in the center of the sleepers, his green eye bright as a direction-finder beacon.

The sun had just hitched itself over the horizon, casting long beams of light through the branches of the trees and dappling the sleeping Harriers with speckles of brightness where they lay in the protection of their screens. The leaves rustled and there was the distant sound of running water. At another time it would have been idyllic.

One of the Mromrosi shook Sventur awake, bouncing on his squat little legs and making a series of high squeaks. "Group Line Chief!" he yelped.

The soporific had worn off enough for Sventur to waken quickly. She sat up, shaking her head, and turned to the Mromrosi, wondering why he had gone all purples. Was she apprehensive because of what had happened so far, or was she responding to a new danger? Not very comforting thoughts first thing in the morning, she told herself as she got to her feet.

"Come at once," he told her anxiously, prodding at her shoulder with one of his eight chubby feet. "Hurry, hurry, hurry. It is very important."

Obediently Sventur got up and put her helmet on as she walked, the visor up. She saw that the others were still asleep.

Except for Group Line Chief Hsuin Xanitan, who lay on his back with a long medical probe protruding from his chest. Crusted blood ran from the wound and formed a puddle beside him, now coagulated to the tackiness of varnish. He had not been dead more than half an hour.

"Pog it all!" Sventur declared. This was worse than anything she had considered. She had supposed if she had escaped one thing, it was the possibility of the murder of her crew.

The other Mromrosi toddled over to them, his curls drooping and his color a washed-out olive shade. "It was very late when this occurred, and I was remiss in my task. There was no sound to alert me, and no movement that I could detect. All I saw was the Bunter tending Group Line Chief Hsuin. I paid no notice until it summoned me to see what had happened."

Sventur hunkered down beside Hsuin, careful not to disturb any detail around him. She drew out her bio-light and ran its beam over the body. The findings were not detailed but sufficient for their circumstances. "Nothing but a stabbing," she said remotely. "No poison, no drugs but painkillers, no organ failure. Just a sharp poke in the chest." She got to her feet, hating herself for what she was thinking.

"It is fatal to your species, I understand," said one of the Mromrosi quietly. "It is a great sorriness."

"When I realized something had happened," said the other Mromrosi, now a gorgeous shade of lilac, "I shut down both the Bunters at once, so that if there is anything in their recall files, it cannot be altered or erased." His manner might have been apologetic for he squnched down, rounding out to the side and reducing his usual one meter height by half and increasing his circumference by a third so that he resembled nothing so much as an enormous furry muffin with a large candied green fruit on top. "I hope I do not offend."

"Thanks," Sventur said without looking away from the body. "You do not offend at all. The recall file is essential. We'll need that."

"A very unfortunate thing," said the other Mromrosi.

"That it is," said Sventur. She looked down at Hsuin's tranquil features. Whoever had killed him had not frightened him. There was no sign of a struggle. Though Hsuin had taken a soporific, a jolt of adrenalin would have shaken it off at once, and he would have been able to fight, if there were danger from an enemy. . . .

"Who got so near him?" Sventur mused aloud. One of the Petits in the ground party must have made it possible for Hsuin to die. That notion was inconceivable, but there was no other explanation.

The flattened Mromrosi was now a ruddy gold shade, and he said, "There was the Bunter and—"

Sventur started to wave this away. "Other than

the—" She stopped herself, and when she went on, it was in another voice. "Bunter!" She rounded on the two Mromrosii. "Yes. You're right. I want the recall files for last night from those two." Her gesture took in both Bunters. "Right now."

"I will wake Parkerman—" offered the Mromrosi as he returned to a more Mromrosi-normal shape.

"No," Sventur countered. "Don't do that. None of the Petits should touch it. Parkerman might be suspect. I want you to do it. If there's any question about the files, I want to be able to show that we Harriers had no chance to interfere with what was on them, and you're the ones who can guarantee that." She also had a sinking feeling that the Bunters might not release the files to her.

"There is truth in that," said the other Mromrosi, his color turning to a very fetching apricot. "Very well, we will attend to it at once." He bounced against his fellow. "Pick one," he said, and added a burst of squeaks and clicks.

The answer sounded like static, but it appeared to satisfy both Mromrosii and they ambled off to do as they had been ordered.

As she stood near the foot of Group Line Chief Hsuin, Sventur looked around the small clearing where they had made their camp, then, as she assessed their position in the light, she went back toward her cocoon. She wanted to get her zap board out before the rest of the camp was awake.

There was some underbrush, she noticed, but

not enough to make approach impossible or too noisy for a skilled assassin. She frowned. As tired as they were last night, and with the soporifics they had taken, it would have required more than a little noise to pull them awake. And with the tracking devices on the various ships, it would not be difficult to find them now that they were stationary.

But there were the Mromrosii on guard—and they were as tired as the Harriers, Sventur reminded herself—and the Bunters.

How could an assassin not alert either the Mromrosii or the Bunters? It niggled at her, that question.

Then she winced afresh at the idea that had taken hold of her. It was unthinkable, that Bunters should do anything against a Harrier, Petit or Grand. Hastily she entered the coded zap and sent it, hoping that the signal would not be detected by the Bastan'gal or the Grands. She tucked the zap board inside her cocoon then folded her arms, lost in thought, and so did not hear as Urthur Mondragon came up to her from behind until his sleepy "You all right, Group Line Chief?" broke through her concentration.

"Mondragon," she said, by way of apology as she turned to look at him. "I guess . . . I'm all right, if you mean healthy. My ankles are pretty stiff, but so are everyone else's."

"Then what is it?" Mondragon asked seriously. "You look sperky, Sventur. Sorry, but you do." He flushed a little, for on Chalot such a personal remark to a superior would earn a stern reprimand.

Sventur scowled. "You'll find out shortly in any case," she said firmly. "It's Hsuin." She looked away.

"He died?" Mondragon changed color almost as dramatically as a Mromrosi—from embarrassed pink to shocked white in half a second. "But he wasn't that badly hurt. How could he die?"

"With a little help," said Sventur. She straightened as she went on, almost as if giving a report. "While the rest of us Harriers were asleep, someone got to him."

"But who?" Mondragon asked, and his question was seconded by Group Chief Miya Maht, her striking Czardas features making her expression of outrage stronger.

"Someone," said Sventur doggedly. "We'll know soon enough."

"You mean someone just came into camp and killed him?" demanded Maht. "Pogger all! How could that happen?"

"Weren't the Bunters keeping watch? Didn't the Mromrosii take guard duty?" asked Mondragon of the tree branches. "How could anyone get here without being noticed."

"I'm hoping to find out," said Sventur testily as she noticed the rest of the Harriers were starting to rise from their cocoons.

"Something's not right," said Maht, and looked toward the closed cocoon where Group Line Chief Hsuin now lay, Protocol Officer Zameda Lauy-Rei standing watch over it.

"Yes," agreed TeRoumei, who had just joined the cluster of Petits at the center of the clearing.

It was very difficult for Sventur to say what she

178

had to say next. "I want both Communication Leaders here, and I want you to record everything we discuss. I want it sent on simultaneous zap, so that there will be a record of it no matter what happens. Otherwise I fear we're going to be forgotten." She started to pace in the confined area the Harriers left for her. "I don't care who has done it, I don't care what the reason for it was, I just want it over. Is that clear?"

There were nods of assent and a few muttered expletives.

"Someone is either after the Harriers in general or the Petits in particular," she said. "So for the time being, everyone stay here, and wait. Have your rations. The Mromrosii will have something for us shortly." It was a promise she hoped the Mromrosii could fulfill.

"And if they don't?" challenged Godwendo.

"Then we'll have to think of something else. Before we move again." She let them think about the danger inherent in that last statement, then added, "So we have to have results of some kind, don't we?"

In less than half an Earth Standard hour the Mromrosii presented Sventur with the tiny spools that constituted the recall files of the two Bunters. One of them was the color of pewter, the other a deep green-bronze.

"We had to use the Emerging Planet Fairness Court over-ride instructions to get these," said the bronze one. "That's why it took longer than we first anticipated it would."

"Thank you," said Sventur, and added, "I want

you to observe everyone in this party when we view the files. Will you do that? And I want anyone detained who attempts to leave. Or arrive, for that matter," she added after a moment.

"If that is what you think best," said the pewter one, and became bluer, more like steel.

"I think it's the only way we can deal with this," said Sventur, hoping she was right.

"Very well," said the bronze one, remaining bronze.

Sventur lifted her hand. "Parkerman. Set up a replay link. Use that expandable screen so that we can all see it."

"The screen isn't very big," Parker Parkerman said as he approached her. "No matter what, I can't get it much larger than the Mromrosii are tall. A square meter's about its greatest expansion."

"Fine," said Sventur grimly. "I want to see these two recall files, the last four days. All right?"

"You mean, from before we arrived?" Parkerman asked, pausing in taking the tiny spools.

"That's what I mean. I want to know who's been issuing the orders." She appeared very serious and Parkerman could not bring himself to question her.

"If that's what you want, Sventur, it's just fine with me." But he cocked his head speculatively as he took custody of the spools as if he did not quite know what to do with them.

"You aren't going to just *play* them, are you?" asked TeRoumei. "Aren't you worried what they might reveal?"

"Of course I am," said Sventur, aware she was answering more of the Petite Harriers than Khirmian TeRoumei. "That's the reason I think we all have to see it at once, or some of you will think that parts were changed or left out or altered." She put her hands together and rested her chin on the tips of her middle fingers. "Whatever is in those files, we'll only find it useful if we see them all at once together."

TeRoumei certainly did not agree. He made the traditional Shimbue gesture meaning hopelessly crazy, then went to lie on top of his cocoon, scorning the protection of its screen.

The steel-colored Mromrosi frowned at TeRoumei, then hopped over toward Sventur. "We have observed the files already," he said. "We will be able to inform you that they are complete."

"Thanks," she whispered, and watched Parkerman assembling his equipment.

In another twenty ES minutes, Parkerman was ready, though he warned that being they were without a full powersource or an auxiliary communications feed they might get poor replay. "We're really tik-tiking here," he reminded all the Harriers. "It's not going to look real good."

"Just get on with it," said Sventur, and was relieved when she saw that all the Petits were gathering closer to the makeshift screen.

"This is Navigator Gos-Raidan's Bunter. The record starts four ES days back, as per orders," said Parkerman, to remind everyone that this long period was not his idea. "We're playing out at five accelerations but we can return to real-time play whenever necessary."

There were more mutters and suggestions, then silence as pictures jerked alive on the screen.

It was the Bunter-zone of the *Yamapunkt*, the walls painted in wide swaths of the ship's colors: green and purple. A dozen Bunters were hooked up to the main Bunter consoles to repower, reprogram and debrief, as they did at least once a day when in space. This particular Bunter was absorbing a reinforcement of one of the basic codes of the Bunters: that the Harriers were to be protected at all costs; that Petits were more expendable than Grands; that the rule of the Fleet Commodore and The Twelve over-ruled the orders of the Harriers. And there was the required provision that the Emerging Planet Fairness Court had access at all times to all records of all actions of all Bunters in the Magnicate Alliance, to be surrendered at once upon submission of the Mromrosii codes. That last had been grudgingly put in after a long, polite negotiation with the six-species EPFC, and it was still regarded by many as dangerous and unnecessary.

Familiar faces and voices flitted by, and the chaos of Line Commander Fayrborn's defection reviewed at high speed except when the Bunters were all forbidden by coding to take no action against Fayrborn—Grands were less expendable than Petits, and Fayrborn had been extended the protective cloak of the Grands—or the Bombard-class ship to which he fled.

Preparation to land on Lontano began, the Bunter keeping with its assigned Petit. Because Korliss Panmix was from Mere Philomene, the Bunter prepared a set of special underwear for the Navigator, as was traditional for any Fille Philomene undertaking important actions.

"I wonder if she still has those on?" asked Ancelott.

Just before the Glavuses left high orbit, there was another dispatch which appeared to be to the Bunters of all the ships.

"We are convinced that this is significant," announced one of the Mromrosii from the rear of the watchers.

The dispatch fed into the Bunter consoles, one that specifically required that the Bunters defend the Grands before the Petits, and to regard any action against the Grands by the Petits as treason, therefore requiring execution out of hand because of their battle status. It was also revealed to the Bunters that the Grands were in the middle of very delicate negotiations with the Bastan'gal, and that any actions against the alien invaders of Lontano would compromise the negotiations beyond repair. Therefore it was essential that any action against the Bastan'gal be viewed as an attack on the Grands as well. The Bunters were to be certain there was no disruption of the negotiative process: the Petits were more expendable than Grands. This was locked with a *most secret* code, and the Bunters returned to duty.

"Soko-pogging-bonocks," whispered Lauy-Rei from her place by Hsuin's body.

Parkerman froze the screen. "That's where the

trouble started, right there," he said, emotion muffling his voice.

The rest were silent, all of them watching intently as the screen once again shifted into rapid motion.

Once Hsuin ordered his ship to attack the Bastan'gal he was regarded as being a dangerous enemy. The recall files made this painfully and abundantly clear.

"I don't think we have to see much more," said Sventur. "Put on the other."

This recall file was from the *Yamapunkt's* Senior Bunter, the coordinator of all the others, responsible for the ship instead of one particular Petit Harrier. It revealed the same pattern, including its coding conflicts that arose when it killed Group Line Chief Hsuin. Its duty was clear. Hsuin was acting against the Bastan'gal, hence against the Grands. But these Petits were the ones the Bunters were coded to protect, and killing them was against that code. The constant conflict between these two incompatible codes brought about such extremity of irresolution that the cyborg came perilously close to experiencing emotion.

"What are we going to do?" murmured Gos-Raidan when the recall file had played out.

"We are going to send those under *most secret* codes and seals to Fleet Commodore Grizmai," said Sventur with authority. "And we will do it very soon. Then we are going to do more, if we can." Watching the screen she had come up with the glimmer of a solution. It might save Lontano, it could keep the J'zmallir Trade Routes from being lost to the Magnicate Alliance, and maybe—if she was very, very lucky—it would keep the rivalry between Petits and Grands from becoming war.

"Our Bunters are back at the ship," said Parkerman thoughtfully.

"So they are," said Sventur.

"Oh, pog it!" said Group Leader Borisov. "No wonder none of us were murdered while we were waiting for you." He stared at Sventur. "Our Bunters' console was shot to pieces and we couldn't get the auxiliary working."

"I thought it was a real problem, having the Bunters out. I was mad about it," said Gos-Raidan. "Can you believe me?" She put one hand to her eyes, and while she did not weep, she did shake. "I can be such a jhum."

There was silence in the clearing, then one of the Mromrosii, who was now a luminous shade of fuchsia, gamboled forward. "Would you mind? We have a suggestion to make."

For nearly a minute there was no sound from any of the Harriers, and then Sventur spoke for them all. "We could use a suggestion or two."

It took until midday to hammer out a rough strategy, and every step of the way there were reasonable objections to offer, but Sventur refused to be turned from her purpose.

"We're short of food, did you ever think of that?" asked Godwendo. "I don't know if I can take any more of those ration sheets, no matter how good they are for me. And liquid-enhancing gels aren't supposed to be used for more than four days."

"And don't say the Bunters can come up with

food," added TeRoumei. "I wouldn't take a deep breath near anything they prepared, let alone eat it." He had this supported by many nods.

"I wouldn't want to chance it myself," said Sventur with real feeling. "I don't think any of us would."

This satisfied the others but did not solve the problem of hunger.

"If you think we can pull this off, then we have to eat." This sensible comment brought emphatic endorsement from the rest.

"We need food and water," said Maht. "We all have Universal Contaminants Blocker pills. We can take them if we have to." She looked directly at Sventur. "You come from here. What's good to eat."

Sventur was about to protest that she had not been here in years and that she had never known the ins and outs of the hearty Lontaniano cuisine, but then something came to mind. "Yeah," she said, as much to herself as to the Harriers waiting around her. "Yeah. I know a place. We can get there in three ES hours if we keep moving. It's a vacation spot. Probably not real busy just now, because of the invasion, but I bet we could get food there, and maybe a base of operations, if we play our cards right." She clapped her hands together. "Right. If we break camp now, we can strike out for Monte Cupert."

Since no one had anything better to recommend, they set about the task as best they could.

"What are we going to tell the others?" asked Communications Leader Parkerman. "They won't know what we're up to if we don't notify them."

"And if we do, every single Bunter from here to The Hub will know where we are," said Ancelott with unconcealed disgust. "You want to risk what could happen next?"

"No, of course not," said Parkerman, his fair moustache bristling.

"We wait until we get where we're going," said Sventur gently. "Otherwise we might as well not go."

One of the Mromrosii, now a deep grape color, added his approval. "It must be assumed that to ask for standard assistance will serve only to increase the chance of open conflict. Therefore as the number and disposition of those opposing you is undetermined but superior to your own numbers, using all reasonable means to minimize that advantage is most genuinely sensible." He sprang into the air. "We of the Emerging Planet Fairness Court do not condone willful recklessness in any species."

"I wonder what that means?" whispered Crozzer as he paused in the act of stowing his cocoon. "Do we have to keep the screens on?" he asked Sventur.

"Yes," she answered. "For now, at any case."

Monte Cupert was called that for its craggy crest of mica-rich dark-red stone that made it appear it was wearing a cowl. At the edge of this magnificent cap there perched a large, white Piedmontese chalet, with balconies and trellises and porticos and cupolas and so many elaborate bay windows that it was nearly impossible to make out the basic U-shape of the building.

Called Elegante Bianc by its owners and Elefante Bianc by the guests, it was a popular and prestigious place to go.

There were—as Sventur had predicted—very few guests staying. It was the slack time of year, and most of the Lontaniani were keeping close to home until the Bastan'gal were gone.

The interior was very like the outside, full of grottos and niches and alcoves and inglenooks. Carpets from Punaraj, Atam Akal, and Kousrau, furniture from Melikos, Vadanao and native Lontano, artwork from throughout the Magnicate Alliance—the lobby alone was better-stocked with treasures than half the museums in the Alliance.

While the hotelier was eager for patrons, he could only manage a sour smile when he saw the bedraggled band of Petit Harriers approaching, dragging two useless Bunters and accompanied by two bright orange Mromrosii.

Sventur went through the ritual greetings and responses as quickly as possible without being outright rude. They exchanged full names and nativity; he was Ernan Radame Foscar, of Gran Rotond. She compared genealogies with the punctilious hotelier only to great-great-grandmothers—they turned out to be third cousins once removed—before she came to the purpose of their visit. Quickly she outlined her plan, hoping that her enthusiasm would win him over.

"We need to have a place where we can control what goes on around us. You can see why your magnificent hotel occurred to me at once," she said, softening the unwelcome information with a compliment.

Foscar was not mollified. "It is hardly convenient to arrange such a function on such short notice, and so irregularly." He indicated the extensive lobby and the lovely view beyond. "We are not designed for the purpose you propose."

"No, but nothing on Lontano is except the Mercantil, and it is in a contested area." Sventur's manner was gracious and polite but there was more than a hint in her attitude that she was determined to use Elegante Bianc no matter what its owner said. "Therefore it is suitable to choose the most renowned of facilities, the most beautiful and impressive."

One of the Mromrosii, a discreet shade of butter-yellow, sauntered up to Foscar. "We of the Emerging Planet Fairness Court would deem it an act of diplomacy and good faith if you were to invite us to hold these necessary meetings here."

The other Mromrosi, a light aqua just now, joined his fellow, green eye beaming beneficently. "It is a wise course, Hotelier Foscar. You may be certain that the various forces caught up in this conflict have discovered where we have come, and without some reason to hold their fire might well decide to attack this place pre-emptively."

That was a threat Sventur had not intended to use, and she heard it with a sinking heart, for she suspected it would turn Foscar against them.

The hotelier pouted and pulled at his elaborate neck-wear—the height of current Lontaniani fashion—but at last performed an elaborate bow. "Under the circumstances, what am I to do but to extend you my hospitality and the hospitality of Elegante Bianc? It appears that either I must assist you or suffer the fate of your enemies."

"Nothing so severe," said Lauy-Rei, unimpressed by Foscar's grand gestures. "You may share the fate of our allies." She made a signal to the rest of the Petits, indicating the lobby and the huge function rooms beyond. "Check them out."

Ancelott and Godwendo took the left, Borisov and Mondragon the right.

"My guests will be displeased with this occurrence," warned Foscar, pointing to the registration clerk. "See? Even the staff is alarmed."

"Your guests will dine out on this tale for the rest of their lives," said Lauy-Rei, dismissing Foscar's objections. "It is a little inconvenience for the chance to witness an historic event. They'll be pleased."

"Pleased?" Foscar exclaimed. "Uniformed soldiers come here and who knows what will follow you. That is not pleasing."

"Then tell them to make the best of it," said Sventur as gently as she could as her patience ran out. "I need to use your powersources. Show them to me, will you?" She almost added the various supplications that ordinarily accompanied a request on Lontano, but she decided against it. She had no desire to become caught up in the tangle of good manners again.

Foscar did not share her feelings, and he gave her an affronted stare. "They are this way," he said with great hauteur, and led her toward the staff sections of the hotel.

This proved to be as spartan as the guest sections were luxurious. Foscar led the way down a steep, narrow staircase, saying as he went, "I don't think I can be responsible for anything that happens to the . . . delegation. You do understand that, don't you?" He addressed not only Sventur but the two Mromrosii who capered along behind her.

"It's on record that we came to you, not the other way around," Sventur assured him. "If anything goes wrong, it'll be my fault."

"And ours as well," one of the Mromrosii assured him.

Foscar sniffed. "Well, at least you understand that." He reached two massive sliding doors. "All our powersources are back here. All I ask is you do not use them all. If anything goes wrong, I want to have something left to run the hotel. I am sure you—"

"Understand," Sventur finished for him. "That I do." She looked up at the banks of cells.

"We operate four funiculs out of here, as well as the hotel," said Foscar as if to explain the tremendous power supply the hotel commanded.

"Those would be the hanging cages we saw as we approached?" said one of the Mromrosii. At the moment he was iris-blue.

Foscar stared at the two aliens in silence for a short while. "I believe I would find your constant change of color disconcerting," he said in his most depressing accents.

"I know," said the other, who was a dull red shade. "It is very amusing to watch your species try to keep us sorted out."

This announcement completely flummoxed Foscar, who could think of no rejoinder and withdrew in disorder, leaving Sventur and the Mromrosii to their work.

"Who first?" asked Sventur, already handing her zap board to the Mromrosii. She pulled the links from their compartment and hooked up the zap board to a third of the powersource.

"We will send ours, so that it is recorded before you begin your action," said the blue Mromrosi.

"And that way there will be no question later about precedent," added the beige one. A moment later he squatted over the zap board and began to operate it with all eight of his three-toed feet.

While the Mromrosii busied themselves with their task, Sventur activated her implant and began to code her first message. What would Fleet Commodore Grizmai think when he discovered she had gone over his head to The Twelve? Nothing she said to him would make amends if he decided she had acted without sufficient justification. It could mean her career. With that cheerless thought to comfort her, she took the zap board from the Mromrosii and began to send her various zaps.

"When do you think you will hear something?" asked Foscar as the Harriers sat in the largest of Elegante Bianc's profusion of bay windows. Below the mountain was glowing ruddy with sunset. "It's been hours."

"We'll hear soon enough," said Sventur with

more certainty than she was feeling. The nearby ships had received her zaps seconds after she had sent them; those going to more distant places would have reached their destinations by now. Little as she wanted to admit it, she was beginning to worry.

"A place like this—it's beautiful, I don't mean it isn't—but . . ." TeRoumei said, wanting to provide a little distraction. "Shimbue isn't like Lontano. A mountain like this . . . we have three hundred seventy-eight active volcanos on Shimbue, and over five hundred dormant ones. On Shimbue you stay away from mountains when you can. There's no way of telling when one might go off."

The others chuckled a little. Even Thorgemann was able to manage half a smile now that he had been properly treated—by an idiosyncratic Lontaniano who actually practiced medicine—and had a decent meal.

"I'm a little surprised we haven't seen any of the Glavuses," said Ancelott, and for once Parkerman took his part.

"Yeah. I've been waiting since noon for one of them. But nothing." He gestured toward the windows. "Fluffy clouds. No Glavuses. No Bastan'gal. Nothing."

It was either a very good or a very bad sign. Sventur could not help but feel the strain, though she was able to mask it with an outward calm that was becoming increasingly difficult to maintain.

"Has anyone checked the vids and surveills in the conference hall?" asked Godwendo. "Lately?"

Foscar paused in the act of pouring more of the heady red wine he had served them with dinner.

"There are alarms on all the screens, vids and zaps," he informed them as if it were the first time someone had asked.

"But still," said Godwendo. "We've been talking. We aren't paying attention."

"Go and check if you want to," said Sventur, as she had every time Godwendo had brought it up throughout the afternoon.

Then one of the Mromrosii scampered forward, going from yellow to pink to a deep violet so quickly that he seemed almost to disappear. "There!" he burst out. "There!"

If the Harriers had not seen Wammgalloz ships before they might have mistaken the armored oddments as flotsam from a battle or part of a wrecked space station.

"Three of them," said Sventur's Executive Officer Duykster. "Three," verified Ancelott, shading his eyes as the peculiar ships drew nearer.

"Where do they think they are going to land?" demanded Foscar, who had just realized the size of the three craft. "This place cannot support such ships. You have to tell them before they wreck—"

The pale Mromrosi approached Foscar. "No, no. You have nothing to worry about. The ships only hover, they never land. Only the Wammgalloz themselves will come here."

If Foscar found this consoling, he did not show it. The portion of wine he poured himself was greater than what he served his guests. "Wammgalloz," he muttered.

The air was humming now, low and tearing, the sound of the ships as they drew near.

"I hate that sound," whispered Sventur's Navigator Estienne Beaumont. "What a noise."

"True enough," said the Navigator of the lost *Suidotal*, Betness Gos-Raidan.

"Everyone up, and in ranks," said Sventur, glad now that she had ordered all the Petit Harriers to do what they could to spruce up their uniforms for this occasion. By all rights they ought to be in dress-5s, not battle gear. She had already politely refused the offer of more appropriate civilian clothing from Foscar and now she was not certain she had done the right thing.

The noise grew louder. Most of the Harriers gritted their teeth as they heard the high, scritchy sound of the Wammgalloz voices above the low growl of their ships.

In their way, the Wammgalloz were magnificent and serene, if it were possible to forget how much they resembled a cross between an Old Earth praying mantis and an older Old Earth Tyrannosaurus Rex. The Wammgalloz had four eyes that took up the greater part of the long pyramid of their heads. They walked on four armored, articulated legs and manipulated things with four telescoping-and-articulated arms. The plating on their very long backs might once have been wings. Of all six species of the Emerging Planet Fairness Court, these were known throughout their sphere of influence for their wisdom and compassion.

Five of these creatures came swaying into the main lobby of the Elegante Bianc, their eyes perilously close to the ceiling. They made their way to the tall rotunda, taking up a position there as if they were a huge ornamental sculpture.

"I had no idea they were so large," said Foscar to Sventur very softly.

One of the Wammgalloz sputtered and hissed; a translator attached to its elongated thorax said mellifluously, "How very kind of you to arrange for this meeting, Petit Harriers, and you Mromrosii."

Sventur saluted, uncertain what else to do, and gave her name, rank and ship. "I'm sorry if this inconveniences you," she added, wondering what the translator would make of it.

"Oh," said the translator of another Wammgalloz after a grating series of clatters and shrieks, "the Emerging Planet Fairness Court exists to be inconvenienced. That is our job." The sound the translators made into laughter sounded like a chest full of rocks and scrap metal being dropped down a flight of stairs.

The Harriers exchanged anxious looks, but the Mromrosii leaped and bounded around the Wammgalloz, the colors of their masses of curls changing rapidly as they did.

"Well," said Sventur, uncertain how to continue. "What do we do now?"

The nearest Wammgalloz bent down so that its tremendous eyes were nearly on a level with her. A terrible scraping sound came from its mouth, but its translator said, "We have summoned all the participants, as you recommended. Now that we have arrived, they should be here shortly."

So that was why it had taken so long for anyone to respond! Sventur could not conceal her satisfaction. "Great. That's great." The translator turned this into a series of high grunts.

After that, no one seemed to know quite what to do.

Foscar tried to fill in by explaining he had nothing in his stores that he supposed the Wammgalloz would want to eat, and even if he had, he had no notion of how to prepare it.

The Mromrosii took over, sashaying between the Harrier and the Wammgalloz, attempting to explain to the five tremendous aliens how they came to be here, starting with the arrival of Group Leader Gernold Willister at the *Semper Rigel.*

"It seemed a fairly simple matter of ending the invasion of a Magnicate Alliance planet," said one of the Mromrosii, curls brightening from mauve to ruddy gold. "The orders were clear enough and well within the rules of the EPFC."

The Wammgalloz listened diligently as the Mromrosii unfolded the story, taking turns and inserting comments in one another's narratives.

"So," the Mromrosi who was green at the moment finished up, "it was discovered that the killer of the Petit Harriers were their own trusted Bunters, acting on their basic codes. They had been persuaded that the Petits had rebelled against the Grands, which is treason in the Magnicate Alliance, and therefore had to be stopped. We have recall files to prove this."

"An excellent source," said the Wammgalloz who had addressed Sventur; she decided that it had to be the leader of the group, if there was a leader.

"And since it appeared that the Bastan'gal were

being protected by some means, we did not know if there would be a way to stop them. But Group Line Chief Sventur has hit upon something that may work. Yes." The Mromrosi bounded into the air, slapped six of his eight feet and landed with a bounce. "Of course," he added as he went from gaudy crimson to forest green, "it won't save the Bastan'gal. But they were Warned."

"Yes," said the apparent leader of the Wammgalloz, "they were Warned."

"Warned?" Sventur echoed, not liking the tone of the word.

The Wammgalloz lowered its head once more. It spoke, like a rake over gravel. The translator said, "The Emerging Planet Fairness Court only Warns once. If the Warning is not heeded, we take the necessary action."

She knew it was very impolite to ask, but Sventur could not help herself. "What action is that?" She could feel the rest of the Harriers listening intently, anticipating a description of annihilation.

"We Quarantine them," explained the Wammgalloz. "None of the species in our sphere of influence are permitted to deal with the Quarantined in any way. No commerce is allowed. No studying is allowed. No exchanges of any kind are possible, direct or indirect. No contact is allowed. If there is contact, then those breaking Quarantine share the fate of the Quarantined. They are contained as well."

"For how long?" asked TeRoumei, his bafflement shared by the rest.

The Wammgalloz pondered its answer. "Going

by your Earth Standard units, the period is no less than thirteen hundred."

"Days?" asked Sventur hopefully, already guessing the answer.

"Years," said the Wammgalloz.

Now that the questioning had begun, the Harriers could not stop. "But why do your . . . sphere of influence planets obey you?" asked Ancelott. "According to the Mromrosii you haven't had a war in thousands and thousands of years."

The Wammgalloz scratched and buzzed among themselves, and then their spokesbeing said, "We do not interfere with what you do among yourselves. That is a matter for the tribunals and customs of the Magnicate Alliance. But when other species are brought in, such as the Bastan'gal, then it is our province. Most of the species in our sphere of influence would rather have an occasional Quarantine than face interstellar warfare. Before the EPFC that happened regularly. Every new species had to battle and claw its way among the other species, and everyone suffered for it. Thousands of planets and systems were wiped out or collapsed. Whole species vanished through aggression and foolishness. The EPFC ended that."

"But if the Quarantined got together—" began Parkerman.

"How?" asked the Mromrosi currently a deep raisin color. "They are blocked from all communication and approach. They are isolated. Even planets within a Quarantined group are not permitted any communication."

"You mean every planet is on its own?" demanded Lauy-Rei.

"Precisely," said the other Mromrosi.

"Even planets in the same system?" asked Godwendo, having trouble grasping the magnitude of Quarantine.

"Even them," said the grey Mromrosi.

"And there has never been a rebellion against this?" asked Duykster, aghast.

"Not recently," said the Wammgalloz, appending, "Not for a very long time."

The Harriers were silent at the thought.

"You force them into isolation? For thirteen hundred ES years?" asked Miya Maht in horrified disbelief.

"Or longer," said the golden Mromrosi.

"Some remain Quarantined for millennia," said the green one. "There is one species, with over two hundred planets in its federacy, that has been Quarantined for nine thousand ES years now, more or less."

"Each planet is isolated from the rest," said Godwendo, to be sure.

"Completely isolated," the gold Mromrosi assured him. "Disruptor beacons are placed in overlapping high orbit around the Quarantined planets. Nothing gets in or out. The beacons are maintained by the Uth-Mah-Dzern and the Ghethept, as they have been from the first."

The enormity of such a sentence was staggering. Even Ernan Radame Foscar was shocked by it.

Finally Sventur asked another question. "How often have you done this—Quarantined a species?"

"In the last eleven thousand years?" replied the Wammgalloz. "Seventeen times."

"You could make it stick?" asked Mondragon, awed.

"Oh, yes," said the Wammgalloz calmly.

"And there was never any trouble about it?" asked Hoad incredulously.

"Not that lasted very long," said the Wammgalloz.

"And no war?" Ancelott inquired.

"Not beyond the species, no," said the Wammgalloz serenely.

Once again the Harriers were silent.

"That is why we have observers on all your ships, as we have on every species' ships with whom we deal," said the Wammgalloz, waving one of its long, telescoping arms in the direction of the Mromrosii. "So that we will have an accurate report on you, and will be able to assess the danger you represent."

Both Mromrosii lolloped down the length of the lobby, their green eyes glowing and their curls a pristine ice-blue.

The Harriers remained silent.

And in that silence an alarm sounded from the central function room where all the vids and surveills had been set up.

The Harriers sprang into action as if freed from a spell and grateful for something to do.

"Parkerman, Ammir, you take charge of communications. Ancelott and Godwendo, guard duty. Crozzer and Porree, I'm assigning you to Foscar, so he won't have to use any of his staff for this. Get to work." It felt good to be giving orders once more, but under the huge eyes of the Wammgalloz she could not help but imagine herself a child in a playground instead of an officer on the eve of what might be a truce.

The Mromrosi who was fading from blue to ecru came up to her, his green eye bright with excitement. "Did you see? The Grands are coming."

"I saw," she answered, her face hardening. Line Commander Fayrborn was on that Petard, the *Mon Droit Cassiopeia*. She was torn by wanting to confront him and by wanting to avoid any confrontation while the fate of Lontano was in dispute.

"What now, Group Line Chief?" asked Thorgemann, who had not risen when the rest did on account of his injury. He was still weak and his complexion pasty, but his eyes were alert and bright.

"I suppose we have to wait," she said, and fixed her eyes on the approaching ship.

Flotilla Master Dunmar Badiban was from Hathaway and proud of it; he was a third son of a second son, but still in the aristocracy and possessed of a title when at home. He had been in the Grands for thirty-two years and was itching for one more real promotion before he retired, one he could parlay into political clout at The Hub as well as on Hathaway. He regarded the group of Petits in the lobby with something close to disgust. "Why have you summoned me here?" he asked, addressing his question to the Wammgalloz as a group.

"There is someone aboard your ship we wish to speak with," said the Wammgalloz's translator. "And there are some questions we wish to ask you."

Badiban contrived to make himself even straighter. "In front of them?" His eyes flicked toward the Petits and then away.

"Certainly," said one of the two Mromrosii.

Seeing Badiban's reluctance, the other Mromrosi said "They already know what is going on, Flotilla Master. There is no reason for you to remain silent any longer."

Badiban's cheeks went scarlet but his manner remained unchanged. "I suppose you think you know what you're talking about."

"Yes, we do," said the Wammgalloz. "And so does the rest of the Emerging Planet Fairness Court." The huge creature bobbed toward Flotilla Master Badiban. "If you will come into the . . . what is this place called?"

"It is the main function room," said Foscar after he cleared his throat.

"The main function room, where the screens are," said the Wammgalloz helpfully. A slow, majestic cocking of its head was enough to impell Badiban forward. "We will sort things out."

Most of the screens were blank, but on one there shone the huge, craggy features of Fleet Commodore Grizmai, who, like most Boreas men, wore a short beard.

"There is a nine-second delay on zaps," explained Communications Leader Parkerman for the benefit of the aliens.

"That is satisfactory," said the Wammgalloz spokesbeing.

"As soon as the others arrive, we will begin," announced the Mromrosii, more or less in unison. They were both a caramel-brown.

"What others?" Flotilla Master Badiban inquired sharply.

"First, your associate Fayrborn, then the commanding officers of the Bastan'gal forces," said one of the Mromrosii, as if the answer were obvious to everyone.

Flotilla Master Badiban was looking seriously displeased. "Whatever for?" he asked, attempting to disguise his apprehension with bluster.

"To answer some questions," said the Mromrosii together. One of them came skipping over to Sventur. "Don't worry," he said quietly, "we'll have this underway shortly."

Since Sventur was not entirely sure what the Mromrosii were up to, she could think of nothing to say.

"You might as well let your Petits relax," the Mromrosi went on. "This isn't official. No need to stand on ceremony for us." He waggled one of his little feet toward the five Wammgalloz and turned a delicious shade of plum. "Most of us don't understand your ceremonies, in any case. We Mromrosii find them amusing, but the rest of the EPFC . . . well, their sense of humor is different."

Sventur would have liked to know what the Mromrosi meant by that but decided she might not like the answer. She folded her arms. "We'd feel better if we continue to stand on ceremony."

The Mromrosi made a gurgling sound, then turned a shimmering acid green. "Whatever you prefer," he said, and capered off in the direction of the other Mromrosi, changing to a rosy shade of apricot as he went.

On the screen next to the face of Fleet Commodore Grizmai there now appeared two of The Twelve—Guei-wan Fampsin of Standby and Chapdean Spiknard of Victoria Station. Both men had well-used, crafty faces and eyes like lancets. Aside from the stamp of their distant ancestries— Korean and Tasmanian—they were as interchangeable as twins. As high-ranking members of the Council of the First Fifty-Six, they had both been born to power and manipulation and by now for both of them the machinations of their high office were as automatic as breathing.

"Will someone explain why we're here?" asked Fampsin, his voice fuzzed with the problems of plus-light transmission.

The Wammgalloz spokesbeing turned to Sventur. "Will you tell them, Group Line Chief? You're the one who arranged this." The translator made this statement seem quiet and polite, but Sventur was not reassured.

She moved forward. "We're not all here yet." She coughed. "You have the zaps I sent?"

In the nine-second delay, she had plenty of time to regret her actions and to convince herself that her actions were bound to fail.

"We have the zaps," said Spiknard. "But they do not entirely explain what is going on there. What are you Petits doing out there in the first place? And why is Flotilla Master Badiban there?"

The silence was longer this time, and finally it

was Fleet Admiral Grizmai who answered. His big face was grim but without anger. "I sent them—the Petits—under most secret codes."

This shocking announcement took Fampsin and Spiknard by surprise and earned a high, squawking yelp from the Wammgalloz which their translators expressed as "Oops" or "Yipe."

Fampsin was the first to recover, for like most Standbyers he prided himself on his inability to be shocked by anything, even if it was very, very odd. "Why did you do that?"

Grizmai mumbled, then hitched his shoulders. "I had to do something. The Marshall-in-Chief of the Grands had been moving ships without informing me, or informing me after-the-fact. I was concerned. I had to know what he was up to."

"So you sent the Petits on a . . . spying mission?" demanded Spiknard.

The Harriers listened, and filled the empty moments between transmissions with whispers.

Flotilla Master Badiban stood rigid, his expression fixed in disbelieving offence.

"On a fact-finding mission," corrected Grizmai when the total eighteen seconds had elapsed. "Unfortunately I chose the wrong unit. I didn't know about Fayrborn's ambitions. They had been removed from his records." His eyes darkened. "I don't know how that happened, but I will find out."

None of the Harriers—Petit or Grand—doubted him.

"Aside from Fayrborn, this was one of the best squadrons of Petits in the service. They were ideally suited to the task, and I knew they would do the job right." He gave a rueful sigh. "I didn't realize the trouble with Fayrborn, or the trouble his associate would cause."

Sventur had been listening attentively but without shock to what Fleet Commodore Grizmai said. But this brought her head up sharply and she gasped. "What associate?"

Flotilla Master Badiban held his breath.

"The review we have given the zaps and the recall files have shown there had to be an accomplice still in the squadron. Someone had to program the Bunters and maintain the program while the mission was in progress." Fleet Commodore Grizmai paused, and went on carefully. "If Group Line Chief Sventur had not sent those zaps, we would never have known what was going on. Fayrborn's associate had been stopping all transmissions back to us. Until yesterday I was totally in the dark about the status of the mission. Then a zap arrived from the *Suidotal*. Sventur sent it. I understand," he went on somberly, "that the Glavus-class skimmer *Suidotal* was destroyed shortly after the zap was sent."

"It was," said Sventur.

"That is all very shocking," said Spiknard when the eighteen seconds had elapsed. As a native of Victoria Station he was expected to be shocked.

Those gathered in the lobby and function room of the Elegante Bianc could only agree.

The Petard *Mon Droit Cassiopeia* was now quite near the Wammgalloz ships, and the signal from the bridge over-rode the plus-light transmissions.

"This is the Grand Harriers Deputy Flotilla

Master Edman Lore of the *Mon Droit Cassiopeia*, responding to orders from Fleet Commodore Grizmai. I have Petit Harrier Line Commander Gilyard Fayrborn aboard." This was Badiban's second in command, a high-born lout from Drought Central.

"We would appreciate it if you would both attend, Deputy Flotilla Master," said the Wammgalloz spokesbeing.

"If that is necessary," came the answer, and then a buzzing of the communications systems as if some interference had been detected.

Two Glavus-class skimmers were approaching out of the west: the *Yamapunkt* and the *Reiwald*.

From the bridge of the *Mon Droit Cassiopeia* Lore could be heard ordering the Petits to stay away.

"Belay that order," Fleet Commodore Grizmai, his transmission at last cutting into the communications between the three ships. "Group Line Chiefs to report to the meeting at once. Deputy Flotilla Master Lore, present yourself with Line Commander Fayrborn. Immediately."

There was no arguing with the Fleet Commodore, and no chance to deny receiving the order.

"Should we have the Mromrosii, as well?" asked the Wammgalloz of Group Line Chief Sventur.

It astonished her to be consulted, but she answered, "Not yet. But have them present you with reports, or whatever they do." She had not yet figured out how it was the Mromrosii relayed their material to the Emerging Planet Fairness Court.

"That is understood," said the Wammgalloz, and rose upward into the rotunda, straightening its back. "Pardon me," its translator remarked. "Bending down for so long is very fatiguing."

"I can imagine," said Sventur, not at all sure this was true.

A few minutes later, Gilyard Fayrborn strode defiantly through the main doors of the Elegante Bianc. He squared his chin and looked at the small group of Petit Harriers who had gathered to watch him. No one saluted.

Beside him, Edman Lore stood with his eyes resolutely forward and his gaze fixed in the middle distance. He slapped his right hand to his left shoulder in the direction of the screens where Grizmai, Spiknard and Fampsin were. "Reporting as per your order, Fleet Commodore," he said, trying not to sound too sycophantish.

"Excellent," said Grizmai, and stared hard across three dozen light-years to Fayrborn. "Well, Line Commander, you have a great deal to answer for."

"Only because I didn't succeed," said Fayrborn, determined to brazen it out. "If I had succeeded, I'd be getting a medal."

"I am afraid not," said the Mromrosi nearest him.

"You were observed," said the other.

Fayrborn gestured as if to push the fluffy, curly aliens aside. "You pogging pests! You make sperks of all of us!"

It was difficult to tell if the Prussian blue the two Mromrosii turned was out of distress, anger or insult, but it was clear that they were mightily displeased. They both turned their single green eyes on him, and one of them hopped into the air—for once it did not seem amusing.

"You are a bigot and a fool," said the Wammgalloz from the rotunda, the sonorous voice of the translator making these condemnations sound less dire. "No force in space can afford such an attitude toward other species."

Fleet Commodore Grizmai looked very displeased, and he addressed the aliens at once. "Gentlem . . . gentlebeings, I ask you not to regard what Fayrborn is saying as anything more than an indication of his overwrought nerves."

"Pogger all!" shouted Fayrborn. "Pog you and The Hub and The Twelve for pandering to these . . . these monstrosities!" He flung the insult at more than the Mromrosii and Wammgalloz in the Elegante Bianc. "And pog you"—he directed this as Sventur—"for your frapping sense of duty. You don't know when to quit." He spat and turned away from her. He wished he had brought a supply of fantod gas with him. It worked once. He might have a chance with another canister of fantod gas.

"You'd better control yourself, Line Commander," warned Spiknard. "You are in no position to make threats."

Gilyard Fayrborn laughed aloud, and the sound was only marginally less unpleasant than the sound of Wammgalloz speech. He glared at the screens, crossed his arms and looked persecuted.

Deputy Flotilla Master Lore was embarrassed by this display and showed it by going a shade of red any Mromrosi would envy.

"From what I have been able to discover thus far," said Fleet Commodore Grizmai, "you, Fayrborn, were contacted by certain high-ranking members of the Grands—your distant relatives, so I gather—for the purpose of gaining control of the access to J'zmallir Trade Routes with the intention of parlaying that access into a power base that would eventually shift the governing power of the Magnicate Alliance from The Hub to the Grands."

Now Fampsin and Spiknard were incensed. Fampsin uttered the ultimate Standby curse— "Hooch palsy and an endless losing streak"—under his breath while Spiknard gathered his hands into fists and pressed them together.

"It will take a while before all the participants in this despicable plan are rounded up," said Grizmai, "but thanks to Sventur's warning, we have a chance to stop this before it gets started."

Warning sirens went off throughout the Elegante Bianc, and now everyone looked around, including those three attending the meeting by vid, though with a nine-second delay.

The three Bastan'gal ships were like half-risen piles of yeast dough. Pale grey in color and with few external markings they came up to the Elegante Bianc sporting yellow-and-white negotiating lights on. They set down on the landing field downslope from the hotel and at once land-craft looking like huge armored moles left the ships and headed up the mountain.

"So," said the Wammgalloz with deep satisfaction. "The matter nears conclusion."

"The Bastan'gal might not agree," said the Mromrosi who was chrome-yellow.

"They were Warned," said the Wammgalloz.

"Yes," agreed the Mromrosi who had turned deep thalo-green.

Sventur listened to this, hoping she had misunderstood what she had overheard, but equally certain she had not.

Fayrborn had become vociferous once more. "I resent this treatment. I do not recognize any authority of the so-called Emerging Planet Fairness Court, and I refuse to be bossed around by *things* like you." He pointed at the five Wammgalloz, then at the two Mromrosii. "It's a sign of our weakness that we let you gain the influence you have. We ought to have stopped it at the beginning."

"Line Commander Fayrborn," thundered Fleet Commodore Grizmai—though some of the impact was lost through the nine-second delay—"you are under arrest, and your associate on the crew of the *Yamapunkt* is also under arrest. You are to be placed in formal detention and delivered to the Marshalls-in-Chief of the Petit and Grand Harriers."

Deputy Flotilla Master Lore coughed delicately. "Fleet Commodore, who aboard the *Yamapunkt* are we to detain? Who is the accomplice?"

Grizmai achieved a tight smile. "Ask Sventur."

Sventur looked horrified, and then realized that she was not implicated. In the same instant, it occurred to her that she knew precisely who had helped Fayrborn, who had the knowledge to alter the codes of the Bunters, who could block zaps and vids and other transmissions, who had to be the Line Commander's accomplice. She was very composed. "Detain Communications Leader Gara Gaikhu," she said.

This revelation brought consternation to all the Harriers, Petit and Grand, in the hotel and on their ships.

"It's never Gaikhu," insisted Group Line Chief Goriz from the *Reiwald*.

Protocol Officer Diam Bontorn of the *Yamapunkt* issued several sharp orders, and then announced, "Communications Leader Gaikhu has been apprehended attempting to flee the ship."

One of the screens that had been blank until that moment now came to brilliant life and revealed Gara Gaikhu restrained by two of the Protocol Officer's staff. She stared defiantly outward. Even angry she was stunning. "You'd better listen to him. He's right. If you arrest him, it won't matter—"

Fayrborn swore savagely.

"—because he will be a martyr and the people of the Magnicate Alliance will flock to his cause. We will not be the pawns of alien martinets."

"Hardly martinets," said one of the Mromrosii.

Sventur looked at the screen where Gaikhu was, trying to puzzle out what had happened to her that she had become Fayrborn's tool. She took a few steps forward. "Gara, how could you . . ." She cleared her throat. "You killed your fellow-Petits. You were prepared to let Lontano be destroyed."

Gaikhu shook her head violently. "They aren't my fellow-Petits. How can you think I'm like

you? Gilyard, he understands. He knows what it
is to be kept out of the Grands on a technicality.
He knows how humiliating it is to be at the beck
and call of those disgusting EPFC species. It has
to change, Leatris. It just has to. Can't you see
that? What's one out-of-the-way planet, compared
to the sovereignty of the Magnicate Alliance."

"Nothing, probably, except it's my home," said
Sventur very quietly, and turned away.

Line Commander Fayrborn fixed her with an
unrelenting stare. "You have a lot to answer for,"
he warned her.

One of the Mromrosii bounded over to Sventur's side and rubbed her side. "Don't worry. The
Emerging Planet Fairness Court knows what
you've done, Sventur."

"Good," said Sventur quietly. "I wish I did."

By the time the Bastan'gal arrived, Line Commander Fayrborn, along with Communications
Leader Gaikhu and Flotilla Master Badiban had
been taken aboard the *Reiwald*, all under orders
to be brought to The Hub by the fastest and
most direct route. They had been guaranteed an
escort of Scimitar-class skimmers to head off any
rescue attempts.

The Wammgalloz had changed the translator
to the voice of the Bastan'gal, and so Sventur
required the Mromrosii to provide her a transla-
tion for the proceedings.

"In the presence of witnesses not members of
the Emerging Planet Fairness Court," the
purple Mromrosi said as the Wammgalloz
translator rendered squeaks, scratches and yips

into low howls and gurgles, "we inform you that you and your entire species are to be placed in Quarantine for your continuing abuse of species other than your own and your illegal exploitation of the J'zmallir Trade Route through piracy and planetary invasion. You were warned two hundred thirty-two years ago and have not heeded our Warning."

The tawny-grey Mromrosi took over the chore. "Therefore you are to be isolated on your forty-six worlds, each population confined to its own world for a period not less than thirteen hundred years. At the end of that time, your situation will be reviewed but not necessarily rescinded."

On the screens Fleet Commodore Grizmai looked distinctly uncomfortable as the Wammgalloz turned their attention from the Bastan'gal to the humans. The translator returned to the deep, melodic voice it had had before.

"There have been offenses on your part, as well. But as the crimes were confined to a small group of rebels within one particular service, you are not yet subject to Warning. However, if the abuses continue, then the Magnicate Alliance will face Warning and Quarantine. For the time being, the actions of your Harrier force, especially the division known as the Grands, will be subject to frequent review and inspection. If at any time it becomes apparent that malfeasance is being tolerated in that force, the possibility of Warning will increase greatly."

The Petit Harriers had gathered together to hear this, and now Ancelott whistled in appreciation.

"You think that would stop the Grands?" asked Godwendo in disgust.

"I hope it would," said Lauy-Rei.

Mondragon watched the Wammgalloz with growing curiosity. "I can't helping wondering if we look as weird to them as they do to us, you know?"

The Wammgalloz was continuing. "Our records will show that your own forces contained the problem before we had to intervene. In fact, the wise precautions of your Group Line Chief Leatris Sventur have done much to mitigate the stigma that would otherwise attach to your species. Your agencies would do well to find more officers like her." The Wammgalloz drew in all but one of its telescoping arms. "It was very well done, summoning us here, Group Line Chief Sventur." It made an attempt to use its one free limb to touch the opposite shoulder, and almost strangled itself in the effort.

Sventur, coming to attention, returned the salute sharply, but out of the corner of her eye she watched the Bastan'gal retreat to their land transportation. In spite of everything, she felt sympathy for them and their plight. She could not read their features but she knew they had to be in profound shock. How would any species react, condemned to isolation on a single planet. She could not imagine living under the terrible conditions imposed on them by the Emerging Planet Fairness Court.

How could anyone, she asked herself, confine themselves to one world, no matter how perfect, and be satisfied?

MISSION OF MERCY

Christopher Stasheff

Thunder cracked as an energy-bolt cleaved air. The blast lit up the port half of the canopy and rocked the ship. Lieutenant Ikeyumi hit the stabilizer sequence, and the shuttlecraft righted itself even as he sent it rocketing back into the stratosphere, swerving in a zigzag path that would have given a nautch dancer a sprained sacroiliac.

"What happened?" Doctor Infarus stammered, pulling himself through the hatchway.

"Some Farmer seems to resent our coming in over the countryside," Sarben answered from the co-pilot's seat. "Must think we're with the Bankers' army."

"You were ordered not to aggravate hostilities!"

"Wrong," said Ikeyumi. "The Commandant ordered us to go down to the Lincoln spaceport and bring back a shipment of pharmaceuticals. He didn't say anything about the hostilities."

Of course, Ikeyumi had known about the war. Lincoln was an agricultural planet in the throes of early industrial development, financed by a consortium of off-planet bankers. Their local representatives were less than scrupulous about how they acquired mineral-rich real estate and land for their factories. The Farmers, who were losing their land as a result, were openly resentful. Very openly, but the Bankers had imported a mercenary army to restrain them. Unfortunately, the Farmers refused to be restrained, and had turned themselves into a top-notch militia.

"Doc," Ikeyumi said between clenched teeth, "get back into the passenger compartment. You're supercargo. Not allowed on the bridge."

"I have a right to know what's going on! I have a duty to the Grand Harriers!"

"Sure, because you are one—but I have a duty to the Petit Harriers, to keep this ship intact. I also might mention something of an obligation to the dozen Petit Harriers aboard this ship."

"The people on New Czerno need that shipment of antiagathol to stop their epidemic! You can't cancel the mission!"

"Oh, can't he?" growled Sarben.

"Can or can't, I won't." But Ikeyumi wished devoutly that he could. "A million people dying from an alien plague is a bit much for even my capacious conscience to hold. But I warn you, Doc, Grand Harrier observer or no, if anybody else shoots at me, I'm going to burn them out!"

"I'm not an observer—just a volunteer! And you can't fire back on them—you'll make the whole civil war flare up again!"

"So let it flare," Ikeyumi growled. "Why're you so big on holding fire, Doc? You've been hinting about it all the way down from orbit."

"Because the Bankers currently hold the spaceport!"

"I know that." Ikeyumi frowned, nodding. "They've announced an embargo, said they'll shoot down any ship trying to land. You mean to tell me they wouldn't even let in a mercy mission?"

"There's a chance they will, a bare chance—but not if you shoot at them."

"If I don't shoot back, I'll come falling out of the sky. But there's more to it than that, isn't there, Doc? Whose side are the Grand Harriers on, anyway?"

"Nobody's side! We're trying to make peace!"

"But just the same, you don't want us to land at the spaceport."

Dr. Infarus turned and looked out at the sky. "The Farmers have an artillery line a mile from the spaceport. If the Bankers let you land, the Farmers will assume you're an enemy. . . ."

"And shoot us down without asking." Ikeyumi turned away. "No contest, Doc. We'll land five miles away and come in by tank."

"It's more complicated than that." Infarus held up a hand. "If you fire on the Farmers, you'll give them cause to start the biggest battle of the war."

"True," Sarben seconded. "They haven't wasted the cease-fire. They've moved up, and their guns are already in place, just waiting for the Bankers to break the truce so they can start shelling the city."

"Why should the Grand Harriers care?" Ikeyumi frowned. "I thought the peace conference was just days away, and both sides were sick of fighting. Okay, so maybe there will be one more battle, but they'll start talking peace again soon enough."

"Maybe," Sarben said. "But if there's one last big battle, it will give the Grand Harriers the chance to appear as the peacemaker and end the war."

"In the Grand Harriers' favor, of course," Ikeyumi grunted. "Of course, the serum and this Petit Harrier expedition will both be lost, but who cares? Not the Grands."

Infarus reddened. "Anyway, you see why it's so important that you not fire."

"No, I see that if I don't, my ship, my crew, and about a hundred thousand New Czerno citizens will die. Yes, Doc, I'll land five miles away and roll in. No, Doc, I won't hold my fire. Any fool that fires on me, is getting my fire back—and if he thinks he can outgun a Petit Harrier, let him try."

They landed in a field five miles away, near a road. Energy bolts exploded near them as they started to descend.

"Fire!" Ikeyumi snapped.

The ship rocked with recoil. An energy bolt exploded a copse at the edge of the field, sending up a fountain of dirt and tree trunks.

"Target neutralized," the gunner reported.

"Going in," Ikeyumi told him.

The Petit Harrier sank toward the field.

A gout of flame blossomed from a rocky outcrop below them.

"Missile coming in," Sarben reported.

"Missile?" Ikeyumi stared. "What's next? Stone axes?"

"Do I fire, Lieutenant?" the gunner demanded, his voice strained.

"Too right you fire!"

A bolt sped out from the ship. Smoke erupted in mid-air, shot with flame, as pure energy met pure foolishness.

More flame blossomed from the outcrop.

"Fire!" Ikeyumi snapped. "And take out the launcher!"

Smoke roiled in mid-air; then the rocks blew apart in a granite rain.

"Hope the artillerymen weren't near their launchers," Dr. Infarus said in a hollow tone.

"Not likely, Doc. Missiles are remoted. Landing gear out!"

Everyone sat in strained silence for a moment. This was the most vulnerable moment—as the ship touched ground. A shell or bolt now would topple them, and it would take long minutes to right the ship. Shells and bolts could rain on them in those minutes, reducing their ship to scrap.

The ground jolted under them.

Ikeyumi sighed. "Secure braces!"

"Secured," Sarben responded.

"Okay." Ikeyumi released his webbing. "Krasno and Belichnai, stay and guard. Everyone else, into the tank. Except you, Doc."

"But I have to come! How will you know which crate to take?"

"I assume it's labelled," Ikeyumi sighed, "but

221

you're right—it might be camouflaged. Okay, let's go."

The ship's side dropped down to form a ramp, and the tank trundled out.

An energy bolt exploded against its port side, rocking it back on one tread. For a moment, it hung balanced.

"Fire port!" Ikeyumi snapped.

The portside cannon snarled, and the recoil knocked the tank back onto its treads. The men inside jolted; then Ikeyumi snapped, "Take out the jughead who shot at us!"

"Targeting," Sarben reported. The tank vibrated as the main gun traversed and elevated; then they all rocked as the cannon spat. Ikeyumi glanced at his viewscreen and saw the gout of earth out near a creek bed. "Got him!"

"Yes, sir." Sarben was grim.

"All right. Up on air, and forward."

The tank filled with thrumming as the huge fans beneath raised the gargantuan machine up a foot off the roadway. There was no sensation of movement, but the scenery began to stream past in the viewscreen.

"Well, we're down and off," Ikeyumi said. "They might be able to assemble more fire power than we've got, or they might not. Not that I care—a plague on both their houses, if they won't let us stop a plague on New Czerno."

Dr. Infarus shuddered. "Please! Just let us Grands stop this war!"

"Fine with me, if you can stop it right now. How did it start, anyway, Doc?"

The doctor shifted uneasily. "Natural clash of

economies and cultures, that's all. The Farmers are the descendants of the original pioneers—farmers and ranchers, mostly, with a few shopkeepers thrown in. But the planet has developed enough to provide an industrial base now. . . ."

"So the Bankers are trying to move in, huh?"

"That's a rather crude way of putting it." Dr. Infarus frowned. "But, yes, the 'Bankers,' as you call them . . ."

"And the Farmers call them, too," Ikeyumi muttered.

"But they're not. Oh, a few of them are bankers, yes, but even they are borrowing development funds from off-planet—funds to buy land for factories, mineral-rich land for mining . . ."

"And the Farmers, for some odd reason, don't like the idea of good fields and pastureland being torn up to gouge out the ore underneath."

"Well, the Bankers resent the Farmers owning all the land, and being unwilling to share!"

"So they talk the Farmers into mortgages, push them into bankruptcy, and take their farms. No wonder they decided to start shooting."

"The Bankers aren't pushing—there just happened to be a drought, until a year ago."

Ikeyumi reflected that, with the technology at its disposal, the Grand Harriers could cause a drought without any trouble. "How odd that the Farmers think the Bankers are a bunch of lying thieves."

"Yes, well, the Bankers sneer at the Farmers for being uncultured hicks—which they are, you must admit."

"Only if you define 'culture' as being the way of life in the cities. Of course, the Bankers aren't too slow to realize that it's easier to take land than to buy it . . ."

"And total up the cost later, and find out that the guns and ammunition and mercenaries cost a good deal more than the purchase price? No, Lieutenant, I think the Bankers would have been more than willing to pay high prices—if the Farmers had been willing to sell."

"They just happen to want to keep their farms."

"You can't stop progress, Lieutenant!"

"Maybe not, Doc, but the Farmers are sure giving it one hell of a try."

A huge crumping sound filled the tank, and the front slammed down, jarring the men against their webbing. Ikeyumi cursed. "What the hell was that?"

"Road mine," a lookout reported. "It got the front fan. Sorry, Lieutenant. I didn't think they'd have any."

"Kill the rear fan! No wonder you didn't think of it, Sergeant—it's really stupid! Mining a road that they both need!" Ikeyumi frowned. "Wait a minute—maybe they saw us coming."

"Sure, the whole planet must know we're coming in, by now. What's that . . ." Sarben stared. "You mean they ran in and set up a mine, just for us?"

"Wouldn't put it past them. Of course, they've put a big hole in their main road, just to stop us, but neither side is thinking about anything sensible like that right now." Ikeyumi shook his head.

"Okay, start up the treads. Full speed as soon as you can—and if anything shows up in the roadway, blast it."

They did. Twice in the next mile, they detected mines and shot them. The explosions blew huge holes in the road, but not big enough to stop the tank's treads.

Ikeyumi shook his head. "Crazy, destroying what they're going to need. Do the Grand Harriers actually think they can stop the shooting, when there's so much outright stupidity on each side?"

"There is a chance, a very good chance." Dr. Infarus frowned, brooding. "Provided we do not disrupt their negotiations in the process of trying to bring back the shipment of vaccine."

Lt. Ikeyumi just sat still for a minute, paying total attention to the amber fields in his viewscreen. Then he said, "Let me get this straight, Doc. You're still trying to tell me that if anybody fires at me, I shouldn't fire back."

"That is what I was hinting at, yes." Dr. Infarus looked relieved. "You've done too much shooting already. We must not do anything further to endanger the chance of peace."

"Do? I'm supposed to bring that serum back right down a battle line, and *I'm* not supposed to do anything to *endanger* it?"

"I'm afraid not, Lieutenant. In particular, you must not do anything to weaken the Farmers— that's vital to cessation of hostilities."

"Wait a minute. The Farmers don't have ways of making any more weapons or ammunition. They're weak enough already—and if we make them any weaker, the Bankers will walk all over them."

"That may be so, but that's not the kind of end to the war the Grand Harriers desire."

"Neither do I—the galaxy wouldn't notice another thousand dead bodies, but I don't need 'em on my conscience. That's not the issue, though, is it, Doc? Where did the Farmers get their weapons from, anyway?"

The doctor's face tightened. "I don't know. Of course I don't know."

"But you suspect, don't you?" Ikeyumi frowned. "After all, how much of a secret could a Grand Harrier keep, aboard its own ship? There had to be rumors, movements seen in the night—or at least somebody commanding, 'Watch the wall, my dear, as the Gentlemen pass by.' Just where are they getting their ammo, Doc?"

The doctor looked away. "I can only speculate, Lieutentant, and that's tantamount to spreading rumors. You know that rumors probably aren't true."

"No, but I'm a natural-born lover of gossip. Speculate a little for me, Doc."

"I have my duty . . ."

Ikeyumi sighed. "Look—if you don't speculate, we might all get shot down. And if we buy the farm, where's your precious shipment then?"

The doctor clamped his jaw shut while he visibly wrestled with himself. Ikeyumi recognized the signs, and waited.

Waited too long. The tank rocked onto its port track; then a huge impact knocked it back onto the starboard.

"Idiots are trying to play ping-pong with us!" Ikeyumi yelled. "Farmers to port, Bankers to starboard! Let 'em have it! All guns! Now!"

The tank stabilized, shuddering, as equal and opposite blasts thundered out of both sides of the vehicle, only slightly out of phase.

"One!" the gunner called out over the booming. "One down! Two! Three down! Four!" He was quiet for a few minutes, then called, "Nothing moving, Lieutenant."

"Damn straight there's nothing moving!" Ikeyumi grinned. "If I were out there, I sure as blazes wouldn't be moving a muscle! Forward!"

The tank ground into motion again.

Something huge swooped down out of the sky.

"Enemy fighter dead ahead!" the lookout shouted.

"Fire!" Ikeyumi bawled.

The main gun filled their world with thunder. The tank rocked back, jounced forward. again.

"Got him!" the lookout crowed. "Only winged—he's swooped up—no, he's stalled . . . he's coming down . . . he's ejected . . ."

On the screen, Ikeyumi saw a dot arcing high away from a meteor that roared down out of the sky, growing larger and larger. . . .

"Dead bird coming straight at us!" the lookout howled.

"Ahead! Full speed!" Ikeyumi hit the throttle before he even started talking.

On the screen, the falling fireball swelled and swelled, then abruptly shot off the top. A huge explosion erupted, knocking the back of the tank high, slewing it from side to side. Ikeyumi held on to the sticks, fighting for control. Their rear hit, and hit hard. The tank bounced once; then it was rolling down the road again, unharmed. The men inside were quiet for a few minutes, listening.

"Anything moving?" Ikeyumi asked.

"Only us," the lookout reported.

They were quiet for a while again, marvelling at survival.

Finally, the doctor said, "Okay. You're right—the Grand Harriers have been supplying the Farmers with weapons and ammunition. But if word of this got out, the Bankers would drop the negotiations faster than a hot rock."

"Yeah, sure." Ikeyumi frowned. "Who's going to listen to a mediator who has been helping the enemy? But something doesn't square, Doc. The Farmers had to have plenty of arms and ammo before they stood up and said 'No' to the Bankers. If they'd known they didn't stand a chance, they'd never have made a try."

The doctor nodded. "That makes sense, Lieutenant."

"What? 'Makes sense?' You're just going to tell me that it 'makes sense?' You can't deny it or confirm it?"

"Exactly, Lieutenant."

Ikeyumi fought down the urge to throttle the man. "Okay, so you don't really know anything, which means you can't say I'm definitely right but I'll settle for 'definitely wrong,' if you know anything that would let you say that. Just for openers, let's say the Grand Harriers were supplying the Farmers with all the ammo they could use, and guns to shoot it out of, before the first shot was ever fired. Could you say 'no' to that, Doc?"

Dr. Infarus reddened and looked as though he were about to say something, but bit it off and managed to stay silent.

"Thought not," Ikeyumi said. "After all, if the Grands had really wanted to end this war, all they would have had to do is just sit back and watch. But they didn't want to—at least, not until it had been going on long enough for everybody to get good and sick of it, and want a way out. Which means that before the Grand Harriers could end the war, there had to be a war."

"Certainly you do not think . . . !"

"No, but you want me to, don't you?" Lt. Ikeyumi watched the doctor through narrowed eyes. "For a smart man, you've been dropping an awful lot of hints. I think that if the Harriers wanted a spy along on this mission, they should have chosen one who didn't care so much about bringing back the serum."

Dr. Infarus's face turned stoney.

"But what's your commission as an officer, against the lives of a hundred thousand people, eh, Doc? Good for you. How about *these* people, though—the Farmer army, and the Bankers' mercenaries who are doing all the dying? What about *their* lives?"

"I couldn't do anything about that," Dr. Infarus snapped.

"Nobody says you could, Doc—except maybe you." Ikeyumi frowned. "Now, why should you think that? Only reason I can think is because you're a Grand Harrier—and you're the sort of noble martyr type who would figure that if the Grand Harriers started the war, and you're a Grand Harrier, then it's your fault for not stopping your bosses."

"It isn't!" Infarus cried in agony. "It can't be! I had no authority, no power to stop them!"

"Good to hear you say it." Ikeyumi nodded. "Even better for you than for us, maybe. Just hope you were listening. You did hear yourself, didn't you, Doc?"

Infarus swallowed and nodded, closing his eyes.

Ikeyumi turned away, gaze roving over the landscape, though he knew his lookout was certainly watching it better than he could. "Now, why should the Grands start a civil war?"

Infarus stayed doggedly silent. The tank rolled along to the steady percussion of the treads.

"Spaceport ahead!" the lookout sang.

Ikeyumi stiffened in his chair. "Be ready! They'll throw everything they've got at us. Gunners, fire at will!"

"Shell at two o'clock!" the lookout shouted.

Ikeyumi swerved. A huge concussion jarred the starboard side of the tank, but it kept on going.

"Eleven o'clock!" the sentry yelled. "Three o'clock!"

Ikeyumi shoved and pulled. Explosions rocked the tank, but it kept rolling, dancing between exploding shells. Then the main gun thundered, and the tank rocked back for a moment before it shouldered ahead.

"Got one of 'em!" the lookout shouted. "Get the one on top of the terminal, Joe!"

"No!" Infarus shouted. "You'll wreck the terminal building!"

"Fire!" Ikeyumi roared. "They should have thought of that before they shot us!"

The main gun spoke again.

"Got him!" the lookout crowed. "Terminal dead ahead, Lieutenant! Do we go out front?"

"We don't bother," Ikeyumi said between clenched teeth. "Main gun horizontal! Fire!"

"No-o-o-o!" Infarus cried, but his wail was lost in the huge concussion that enwrapped them. Smoke filled the viewscreen.

"Shell coming in at twelve o'clock!" the lookout called.

"Side guns, fire!" Ikeyumi snapped.

A double explosion deafened them.

"Got it!" the lookout reported.

The smoke cleared on the screen, showing a huge ragged hole in the side of the terminal.

"Going in!" Ikeyumi warned.

The tank jounced and jostled, canting thirty degrees to port, twenty to starboard—but it kept on going, grinding on in.

"Pop the hatch!" Ikeyumi released his safety harness. "Let's go, Doc! Gunners, cover! They're going to be waiting with every small arm they've got!"

"How about we announce you?" Joe suggested.

Ikeyumi nodded. "Hand 'em our calling card."

The tank was filled with the racheting of a heavy machine gun, mounted just overhead.

"Now!" Ikeyumi vaulted out of the hatch a heartbeat after the machine gun went silent. White-faced, Infarus followed him.

They leaped out, dropped down the side of the tank. Small arms fire began to crackle all around them. Machine guns chattered.

The racheting began again, from the top of the tank. The side guns boomed, sending shells into the corners of the ramps and balconies where the snipers lodged.

The enemy guns went silent.

"Start here!" Ikeyumi darted over to a pile of crates. "Guns!" He heaved the first crate aside, saw the silhouette on the plastic underneath. "Ammo!" He kicked it away. "Chocolate?!"

"Here it is!" Infarus came up with a small crate hugged to his chest.

Ikeyumi stared. "Where are the rest?"

"Just the one! All we really need is a cup of serum, and we can mass-produce batches from it! This box must hold a gallon!"

"Then let's go!" Ikeyumi started back toward the tank, running.

A slug slapped the concrete a foot in front of his boots, ricocheting. Ikeyumi jumped and cursed. The tank's side-gun barked. Far away, someone screamed.

"Let's go, Doc!" Ikeyumi called.

Another sniper's gun cracked, and Infarus yelled incoherently. The side gun spoke, and something thudded. Ikeyumi turned back.

Infarus was down, blood spreading over his thigh. "Go without me!" he gasped. "I don't matter—only the serum!"

"Don't be ridiculous!" Ikeyumi snapped. "Hold tight to that box!" He braced himself and hauled the doctor up to his shoulder in one quick surge, in a fireman's carry. Infarus clung to the crate for dear life.

Ikeyumi turned and trotted back to the side of the tank. Gunfire rang around his feet, but the side gun spoke again, and it stopped. He came to the tank and eased Infarus down onto one of the treads. "Give me the box, Doc."

Infarus surrendered the crate.

"Up here, Lieutenant!" Sarben reached down out of the hatch.

"Brace yourself, Doc." Ikeyumi boosted the doctor back up to the hatch. Teeth gritted, Infarus let himself be hauled aboard like a side of beef. Ikeyumi followed him.

The terminal was oddly silent behind him.

He strapped himself into his chair. Infarus half-lay beside him, face pale, breath ragged.

"Missed the artery by a quarter of an inch," Sarben finished securing a bandage. "I hit him with a pain-killer." He scrambled back into his seat. "Should be taking effect any time now."

"All right." Ikeyumi set his jaw and started turning the tank. "Back we go, back down the gamut."

"They're going to have everything and its brother waiting for us by now, Lieutenant," Sarben warned.

"I know," Ikeyumi said grimly.

"Bogey at five o'clock!" the lookout sang.

"Five?" Ikeyumi looked up. "Behind us?"

"Eagle to egg," the radio called. "Come in, Lieutenant."

Ikeyumi stared, then called back, "Egg to eagle! What the hell are you doing aloft, Krasno?"

"It seemed like a good idea at the time, Lieutenant. They ranged heavy guns on us, so we took off and dropped a few shells on them. Then as long as we were up, I thought we might as well do the same to the spaceport guns, too."

"The spaceport defense bunkers! Are you crazy? You'll get shot down trying!"

"Shot down? Lieutenant, you took out every artillery nest all the way in! Nothing to hammer us now, except right on the tarmac—and we already blew out one of those!"

A huge concussion shook the terminal.

"Make that two," the radio amended. "Meet you out on the pavement, Lieutenant."

They did.

Ikeyumi sat beside Infarus's bed in the Petit Harrier infirmary, with Sarben beside him. "I got to hand it to you, Doc. You had the sand, when the chips were down."

"Mixed metaphor?" Infarus grunted.

"Depends on the kind of chips."

Infarus smiled. "But I'll be back aboard a Grand Harrier ship tomorrow. You realize I can't tell you anything."

"Yeah, but you don't have to," Ikeyumi mused. "I said it myself already, didn't I? The Grand Harriers can't be the hero who bails them out, if the boat isn't already sinking. Start a civil war, keep it going until everybody's good and sick of it, then come riding in and play peacemaker. But that's not all there is to it, is there, Doc? Or the Grands wouldn't have been so big about not hurting the Farmers—and that is one thing they told you to give me orders about, isn't it? Shoot the Bankers, but don't shoot the poor underdog Farmers. Of course, if our expedition should just happen to have weakened the Bankers enough for the Farmers to be in the stronger position at the peace conference, they'd be so indebted to the Grand Harriers that they would be virtually a puppet government, willing to grant all sorts of concessions, making the planet an ideal refitting and refueling base. What started the war, anyway? We know what led up to it, but we don't know what triggered the opening salvo. Wouldn't have any idea, would you, Doc?"

"I would," Sarben said, thin-lipped.

Ikeyumi turned to him with a frown. "Why should you care?"

"'Cause my home planet's a lot like this one. I come from farm folks, myself—and if the Grands can do it to this planet, they can do it to mine, too."

"So." Ikeyumi's eyes glittered. "What did they do?"

"They ended the drought, started buying grain at hugely inflated prices, and paid in gold. Lots of gold."

Ikeyumi grinned. "The Bankers must have loved that."

"Oh, you bet! Operating on a gold standard, and suddenly seeing gold inflation? Losing a dollar an ounce a day? When the farmers started paying off their mortgages with cheap gold, and the Bankers realized they were not only going to lose money, but also weren't going to get any more real estate, they passed a law forbidding the importation of gold. The Farmers raised unholy hell, claiming they hadn't been represented, but the Bankers were in no mood to negotiate. They just called in the mercenaries."

"And the Farmers used all their new gold to buy arms and ammo from the Grand Harriers," Ikeyumi mused, "so the Grands even got their gold back. Neat, very neat."

"But we didn't weaken the Farmers for them," Sarben told Infarus.

Ikeyumi nodded. "We fired on both sides, with great impartiality and fairness—and the result is, they both hate our guts. Then, as we took off, both sides fired at us, but they didn't have any guns left close enough to do us any damage."

"Except for one shot," Sarben amended. "Knocked off a few skin tiles. Took two hours to secure new ones."

"Heavy casualties," Infarus said, with irony. "Who winged us? Farmers, or Bankers?"

Ikeyumi grinned. "Who cares?"

No one, as it turned out—least of all, the Bankers and Farmers, who, united by the common enemy of a Petit Harrier, quickly formed a coalition government to resist all off-planet invasions. They compared notes and discovered that both gold and guns had been coming from the Grand Harriers. The Farmers felt used, and the Bankers felt assaulted; both agreed on barring the Grand Harriers from the planet.

The Grand Harriers took offense and sent down a landing craft to teach them better manners. Both sides together blasted it out of the sky.

This was not much consolation to Infarus, who was cashiered for incompetence. Oh, he had prevented a plague—it made it worse that it had been a Petit Harrier that had taken him to New Czerno with the serum—but he hadn't made Ikeyumi's expedition weaken the Bankers the way his bosses had planned. He was stripped of rank and drummed out of the Grand Harriers in a very impressive ceremony. He felt very badly about it—until Ikeyumi signed him on. All in all, he felt much better being a doctor in the Petit Harriers. Better doctor, but a better Harrier, too.

An excerpt from MAN-KZIN WARS II, created by *Larry Niven*:

The Children's Hour

Chuut-Riit always enjoyed visiting the quarters of his male offspring.

"What will it be this time?" he wondered, as he passed the outer guards.

The household troopers drew claws before their eyes in salute, faceless in impact-armor and goggled helmets, the beam-rifles ready in their hands. He paced past the surveillance cameras, the detector pods, the death-casters and the mines; then past the inner guards at their consoles, humans raised in the household under the supervision of his personal retainers.

The retainers were males grown old in the Riit family's service. There had always been those willing to exchange the uncertain rewards of competition for a secure place, maintenance, and the odd female. Ordinary kzin were not to be trusted in so sensitive a position, but these were families which had served the Riit clan for generation after generation. There was a natural culling effect; those too ambitious left for the Patriarchy's military and the slim chance of advancement, those too timid were not given opportunity to breed.

Perhaps a pity that such cannot be used outside the household, Chuut-Riit thought. Competition for rank was far too intense and personal for that, of course.

He walked past the modern sections, and into an area that was pure Old Kzin; maze-walls of reddish sandstone with twisted spines of wrought-iron on their tops, the tips glistening razor-edged. Fortress-architecture from a world older than this, more massive, colder and drier; from a planet harsh enough that a plains carnivore had changed its ways, put to different use an upright posture designed to place its head above savanna grass, grasping paws evolved to climb rock. Here the modern features were reclusive, hidden in wall and buttress. The door was a hammered slab graven with the faces of night-hunting beasts, between towers five times the height of a kzin. The air smelled of wet rock and the raked sand of the gardens.

Chuut-Riit put his hand on the black metal of the outer portal, stopped. His ears pivoted, and he blinked; out of the corner of his eye he saw a pair of tufted eyebrows glancing through the thick twisted metal on the rim of the ten-meter battlement. *Why, the little sthondats,* he thought affectionately. *They managed to put it together out of reach of the holo pickups.*

The adult put his hand to the door again, keying the locking sequence, then bounded backward four times his own length from a standing start. Even under the lighter gravity of Wunderland, it was a creditable feat. And necessary, for the massive panels rang and toppled as the rope-swung boulder slammed forward. The children had hung two cables from either tower, with the rock at the point of the V and a third rope to draw it back. As the doors bounced wide he saw the blade they had driven into the apex of the egg-shaped granite rock, long and barbed and polished to a wicked point.

Kittens, he thought. *Always going for the dramatic.* If that thing had struck him, or the doors under its impetus had, there would have been no need of a blade. *Watching too many historical adventure holos.* "Errorowwww!" he shrieked in mock-rage bounding through the shattered portal and into the interior court, halting atop the kzin-high boulder. A round dozen of his older sons were grouped behind the rock, standing in a defensive clump and glaring at him, the crackly scent of their excitement and fear made the fur bristle along his spine. He glared until they dropped their eyes, continued it until they went down on their stomachs, rubbed their chins along the ground and then rolled over for a symbolic exposure of the stomach.

"Congratulations," he said. "That was the closest you've gotten. Who was in charge?"

More guilty sidelong glances among the adolescent males crouching among their discarded pull-rope, and then a lanky youngster with platter-sized feet and hands came squatting-erect. His fur was in the proper flat posture, but the naked pink of his tail still twitched stiffly.

"I was," he said keeping his eyes formally down. "Honored Sire Chuut-Riit," he added, at the adult's warning rumble.

"Now, youngling, What did you learn from your first attempt?"

"That no one among us is your match, Honored Sire Chuut-Riit," the kitten said. Uneasy ripples went over the black-striped orange of his pelt.

"And what have you learned from this attempt?"

"That all of us together are no match for you, Honored Sire Chuut-Riit," the striped youth said.

"That we didn't locate all of the cameras," another muttered. "You idiot, Spotty." That to one of his siblings; they snarled at each other from their crouches, hissing past barred fangs and making striking motions with unsheathed claws.

"No, you did locate them all, cubs," Chuut-Riit said. "I presume you stole the ropes and tools from the workshop, prepared the boulder in the ravine in the next courtyard, then rushed to set it all up between the time I cleared the last gatehouse and my arrival?"

Uneasy nods. He held his ears and tail stiffly, letting his whiskers quiver slightly and holding in the rush of love and pride he felt, more delicious than milk heated with bourbon. *Look at them!* he thought. At the age when most young kzin were helpless prisoners of instinct and hormone, wasting their strength ripping each other up or making fruitless direct attacks on their sires, or demanding to be allowed to join the Patriarchy's service *at once* to win a Name and household of their own . . . *His* get had learned to *cooperate* and use their minds!

"Ah, Honored Sire Chuut-Riit, we set the ropes up beforehand, but made it look as if we were using them for tumbling practice," the one the others called Spotty said. Some of them glared at him, and the adult raised his hand again.

"No, no, I am *moderately* pleased." A pause. "You did not hope to take over my official position if you had disposed of me?"

"No, Honored Sire Chuut-Riit," the tall leader said. There had been a time when any kzin's holdings were the prize of the victor in a duel, and the dueling rules were interpreted more leniently for a young subadult. Everyone had a sentimental streak for a successful youngster; every male kzin remembered the intolerable stress of being physically mature but remaining under dominance as a child.

Still, these days affairs were handled in a more civilized manner. Only the Patriarchy could award military and political office. And this mass assassination attempt was . . . unorthodox, to say the least. Outside the rules more because of its rarity than because of formal disapproval. . . .

A vigorous toss of the head. "Oh, no, Honored Sire Chuut-Riit. We had an agreement to divide the private possessions. The lands and the, ah, females." Passing their own mothers to half-siblings, of course. "Then we wouldn't each have so much we'd get too many challenges, and we'd agreed to help each other against outsiders," the leader of the plot finished virtuously.

"Fatuous young scoundrels," Chuut-Riit said. His eyes narrowed dangerously. "You haven't been communicating outside the household, have you?" he snarled.

"Oh, *no*, Honored Sire Chuut-Riit!"

"Word of honor! May we die nameless if we should do such a thing!"

The adult nodded, satisfied that good family feeling had prevailed. "Well as I said, I am somewhat pleased. If you have been keeping up with your lessons. Is there anything you wish?"

"Fresh meat, Honored Sire Chuut-Riit," the spotted one said. The adult could have told him by the scent, of course, a kzin never forgot another's personal odor, that was one reason why names were less necessary among their species. "The reconstituted stuff from the dispensers is always . . . so . . . *quiet*."

Chuut-Riit hid his amusement. Young Heroes-to-be were always kept on an inadequate diet, to increase their aggressiveness. A matter for careful gauging, since too much hunger would drive them into mindless cannibalistic frenzy.

"And couldn't we have the human servants back? They were nice." Vigorous gestures of assent. Another added: "They told good stories. I miss my Clothilda-human."

"Silence!" Chuut-Riit roared. The youngsters flattened stomach and chin to the ground again. "Not until you can be trusted not to injure them; how many times do I have to tell you, it's dishonorable to attack household servants! Until you learn self-control, you will have to make do with machines."

This time all of them turned and glared at a mottled youngster in the rear of their group; there were half-healed scars over his head and shoulders. "It bared its *teeth* at me," he said sulkily. "All I did was swipe at it, how was I supposed to know it would die?" A chorus of rumbles, and this time several of the covert kicks and clawstrikes landed.

"Enough," Chuut-Riit said after a moment. *Good, they have even learned how to discipline each other as a unit.* "I will consider it, when all of you can pass a test on the interpretation of human expressions and body-language." He drew himself up. "In the meantime, within the next two eight-days, there will be a formal hunt and meeting in the Patriarch's Preserve; kzinti homeworld game, the best Earth animals, and even some feral-human outlaws, perhaps!"

He could smell their excitement increase, a mane-crinkling musky odor not unmixed with the sour whiff of fear. Such a hunt was not without danger for adolescents, being a good opportunity for hostile adults to cull a few of a hated rival's offspring with no possibility of blame. *They will be in less danger than most,* Chuut-Riit thought judiciously. *In fact, they may run across a few of my subordinates' get and mob them. Good.*

"And if we do well, afterwards a feast and a visit to the Sterile Ones." That had them all quiveringly alert, their tails held rigid and tongues lolling; nonbearing females were kept as a rare privilege for Heroes whose accomplishments were not *quite* deserving of a mate of their own. Very rare for kits still in the household to be granted such, but Chuut-Riit thought it past time to admit that modern society demanded a prolonged adolescence. The day when a male kit could be given a spear, a knife, a rope and a bag of salt and kicked out the front gate at puberty were long gone. Those were the wild, wandering years in the old days, when survival challenges used up the superabundant energies. Now they must be spent learning history, technology, xenology, none of which burned off the gland-juices saturating flesh and brain.

He jumped down amid his sons, and they pressed around him, purring throatily with adoration and fear and respect;

his presence and the failure of their plot had reestablished his personal dominance unambiguously, and there was no danger from them for now. Chuut-Riit basked in their worship, feeling the rough caress of their tongues on his fur and scratching behind his ears. *Together*, he thought. *Together we will do wonders.*

From "The Children's Hour" by Jerry Pournelle & S.M. Stirling

THE MAN-KZIN WARS
72076-7 • 304 pages • $5.99   _____

MAN-KZIN WARS II
72036-8 • 320 pages • $4.99   _____

MAN-KZIN WARS III
72008-2 • 320 pages • $4.99   _____

MAN-KZIN WARS IV
72079-1 • 352 pages • $4.95   _____

MAN-KZIN WARS V
72137-2 • 288 pages • $5.99   _____

These bestsellers are available at your local book-store, or just send this coupon, your name and address, and the cover price(s) to: Baen Books, Dept. BA, P.O. Box 1403, Riverdale, NY 10471.

JOHN DALMAS

He's done it all!

John Dalmas has just about done it all—parachute infantryman, army medic, stevedore, merchant seaman, logger, smokejumper, administrative forester, farm worker, creamery worker, technical writer, free-lance editor—and his experience is reflected in his writing. His marvelous sense of nature and wilderness combined with his high-tech world view involves the reader with his very real characters. For lovers of fast-paced action-adventures!

THE REGIMENT
The planet Tyss is so poor that it has only one resource: its fighting men. Each year three regiments are sent forth into the galaxy. And once a regiment is constituted, it never recruits again: as casualties mount the regiment becomes a battalion ... a company ... a platoon ... a squad ... and then there are none. But after the last man of *this* regiment has flung himself into battle, the Federation of Worlds will never be the same!

THE WHITE REGIMENT
All the Confederation of Worlds wanted was a little peace. So they applied their personnel selection technology to war and picked the greatest potential warriors out of their planets-wide database of psych profiles. And they hired the finest mercenaries in the galaxy to train the first test regiment—they hired the legendary black warriors of Tyss to create the first ever White Regiment.

THE KALIF'S WAR
The White Regiment had driven back the soldiers of the Kharganik empire, but the Kalif was certain that

he could succeed in bringing the true faith of the Prophet of Kargh to the Confederation—even if he had to bombard the infidels' planets with nuclear weapons to do it! But first he would have to thwart a conspiracy in his own ranks that was planning to replace him with a more tractable figurehead . . .

FANGLITH
Fanglith was a near-mythical world to which criminals and misfits had been exiled long ago. The planet becomes all too real to Larn and Deneen when they track their parents there, and find themselves in the middle of the Age of Chivalry on a world that will one day be known as Earth.

RETURN TO FANGLITH
The oppressive Empire of Human Worlds, temporarily filed in *Fanglith*, has struck back and resubjugated its colony planets. Larn and Deneen must again flee their home. Their final object is to reach a rebel base—but the first stop is Fanglith!

THE LIZARD WAR
A thousand years after World War III and Earth lies supine beneath the heel of a gang of alien sociopaths who like to torture whole populations for sport. But while the 16th century level of technology the aliens found was relatively easy to squelch, the mystic warrior sects that had evolved in the meantime weren't. . . .

THE LANTERN OF GOD
They were pleasure droids, designed for maximum esthetic sensibility and appeal, abandoned on a deserted planet after catastrophic systems failure on their transport ship. After 2000 years undisturbed, "real" humans arrive on the scene—and 2000 thousand years of droid freedom is about to come to a sharp and bloody end.

THE REALITY MATRIX

Is the existence we call life on Earth for real, or is it a game? Might Earth be an artificial construct designed by a group of higher beings? Is everything an illusion? Everything is—except the Reality Matrix. And what if self-appointed "Lords of Chaos" place a chaos generator in the matrix, just to see what will happen? Answer: The slow destruction of our world.

THE GENERAL'S PRESIDENT

The stock market crash of 1994 makes Black Monday of 1929 look like a minor market adjustment—and the fabric of society is torn beyond repair. The Vice President resigns under a cloud of scandal—and when the military hints that they may let the lynch mobs through anyway, the President resigns as well. So the Generals get to pick a President. But the man they choose turns out to be more of a leader than they bargained for....

Available at your local bookstore. Or you can order any or all of John Dalmas' books with this order form. Just check your choice(s) below and send the combined cover price to: Baen Books, Dept. BA, P.O. Box 1403, Riverdale, NY 10471.

THE REGIMENT • 416 pp. • 72065-1 • $4.95   _____

THE WHITE REGIMENT • 416 pp. • 69880-X • $4.99   _____

THE KALIF'S WAR • 416 pp. • 72062-7 • $4.95   _____

FANGLITH • 256 pp. • 55988-5 • $2.95   _____

RETURN TO FANGLITH • 288 pp. • 65343-1 • $2.95   _____

THE LIZARD WAR • 320 pp. • 69851-6 • $4.99   _____

THE LANTERN OF GOD • 416 pp. • 69821-4 • $3.95   _____

THE REALITY MATRIX • 352 pp. • 65583-3 • $2.95   _____

THE GENERAL'S PRESIDENT • 384 pp. • 65384-9 • $3.50   _____

PRAISE FOR
LOIS MCMASTER BUJOLD

What the critics say:

The Warrior's Apprentice: "Now here's a fun romp through the spaceways—not so much a space opera as space ballet.... it has all the 'right stuff.' A lot of thought and thoughtfulness stand behind the all-too-human characters. Enjoy this one, and look forward to the next."   —Dean Lambe, *SF Reviews*

"The pace is breathless, the characterization thoughtful and emotionally powerful, and the author's narrative technique and command of language compelling. Highly recommended."   —*Booklist*

Brothers in Arms: "... she gives it a geniune depth of character, while reveling in the wild turnings of her tale.... Bujold is as audacious as her favorite hero, and as brilliantly (if sneakily) successful."   —*Locus*

"Miles Vorkosigan is such a great character that I'll read anything Lois wants to write about him.... a book to re-read on cold rainy days." —Robert Coulson, *Comics Buyer's Guide*

Borders of Infinity: "Bujold's series hero Miles Vorkosigan may be a lord by birth and an admiral by rank, but a bone disease that has left him hobbled and in frequent pain has sensitized him to the suffering of outcasts in his very hierarchical era.... Playing off Miles's reserve and cleverness, Bujold draws outrageous and outlandish foils to color her high-minded adventures."   —*Publishers Weekly*

Falling Free: "In *Falling Free* Lois McMaster Bujold has written her fourth straight superb novel. ... How to break down a talent like Bujold's into analyzable components? Best not to try. Best to say 'Read, or you will be missing something extraordinary.' " —Roland Green, *Chicago Sun-Times*

The Vor Game: "The chronicles of Miles Vorkosigan are far too witty to be literary junk food, but they rouse the kind of craving that makes popcorn magically vanish during a double feature."   —Faren Miller, *Locus*

MORE PRAISE FOR
LOIS MCMASTER BUJOLD

What the readers say:

"My copy of *Shards of Honor* is falling apart I've reread it so often.... I'll read whatever you write. You've certainly proved yourself a grand storyteller."
—Liesl Kolbe, Colorado Springs, CO

"I experience the stories of Miles Vorkosigan as almost viscerally uplifting.... But certainly, even the weightiest theme would have less impact than a cinder on snow were it not for a rousing good story, and good storytelling with it. This is the second thing I want to thank you for.... I suppose if you boiled down all I've said to its simplest expression, it would be that I immensely enjoy and admire your work. I submit that, as literature, your work raises the overall level of the science fiction genre, and spiritually, your work cannot avoid positively influencing all who read it."
—Glen Stonebraker, Gaithersburg, MD

" 'The Mountains of Mourning' [in *Borders of Infinity*] was one of the best-crafted, and simply best, works I'd ever read. When I finished it, I immediately turned back to the beginning and read it again, and I can't remember the last time I did that."   —Betsy Bizot, Lisle, IL

"I can only hope that you will continue to write, so that I can continue to read (and of course buy) your books, for they make me laugh and cry and think ... rare indeed."   —Steven Knott, Major, USAF

What do you say?

Send me these books!

Shards of Honor 72087-2 $4.99 _____
The Warrior's Apprentice 72066-X $4.50 _____
Ethan of Athos 65604-X $4.99 _____
Falling Free 65398-9 $4.99 _____
Brothers in Arms 69799-4 $4.99 _____
Borders of Infinity 69841-9 $4.99 _____
The Vor Game 72014-7 $4.99 _____
Barrayar 72083-X $4.99 _____
The Spirit Ring (hardcover) 72142-9 $17.00 _____

Lois McMaster Bujold:
Only from Baen Books

*If these books are not available at your local bookstore, just
check your choices above, fill out this coupon and send a
check or money order for the cover price to Baen Books, Dept.
BA, P.O. Box 1403, Riverdale, NY 10471.*

NAME: _____

ADDRESS: _____

_____

I have enclosed a check or money order in the amount
of $ _____.

DAVID DRAKE
HAMMER'S
Slammers

The meanest bunch
of mercs who ever
killed a world for pay—
only from Baen Books!

Hammer's Slammers—The original! Plus—an all-new short novel, "The Tank Lords."
69867-2 • 288 pages • $4.95 ☐

At Any Price—The 23rd-century armored division faces its deadliest enemies ever: aliens who *teleport* into combat.
55978-8 • 288 pages • $4.95 ☐

Counting the Cost—The toughest mission in their history: can the Slammers do it? Not if they abide by the rules of civilized warfare . . . but nobody ever said the Slammers were *nice*.
63955-5 • 288 pages • $4.95 ☐

Rolling Hot—They've got 300 miles of hostile territory to cover, fighting all the way. Their chances are not good—but those who oppose them have no chance at all, because war-worn and battle-crazed as they may be, they *are* Slammers, and they are *Rolling Hot*.
69837-0 • 329 pages • $4.50 ☐

The Warrior—They were the best. Colonel Alois Hammer welded five thousand individual killers into a weapon more deadly than any other in the human universe. But different styles of being "the best" meant a bloodbath, even by the grim standards of *Hammer's Slammers*.
72058-9 • 288 pages • $4.95 ☐

Available at your local bookstore, or send this coupon, your name, your address, and the cover price(s) to Baen Books, Dept. BA, P.O. Box 1403, Riverdale, NY 10471.